Foul play

'He was seated at the desk, as if in readiness for the start of the scene but, instead of leaning back in his chair so that as the curtains opened the audience would see the front of his blood-stained shirt, he was lying slumped forward across its surface, one arm dangling loose, the fingers brushing the carpet, the other spread wide across the top of the desk . . . What a hell of a time to choose to pass out!'

But this was no summit of the actor's art; this death was for real.

A stage adaptation of the best-known novel of G. B. Russell, a celebrated detective novelist of the '20s and '30s, is the high point of the writer's Centenary Festival in the grounds of Cressetts, a bewitching country mansion in East Anglia.

Russell's grandson, Oliver Hampden, a power-hungry charmer, by many loved and feared in equal proportions, is the central figure in a drama in which reality steals the show, providing Detective Chief Inspector Jack Finch with a murder investigation and a final confrontation with the killer which puts his own life at risk.

Sexual jealousy, social ambition and revenge fuel the rivalries and passions of a disparate cast in this tense tale by a matchless storyteller.

FOUL PLAY

June Thomson

Constable · London

First published in Great Britain 1991
by Constable & Company Ltd
3 The Lanchesters, 162 Fulham Palace Road
London W6 9ER
Copyright © 1991 by June Thomson
The right of June Thomson to
be identified as the author of this work
has been asserted by her in accordance
with the Copyright, Designs and Patents Act 1988
ISBN 0 09 470710 3
Set in Linotron 10pt Palatino
and printed in Great Britain by Redwood Press Limited
Melksham, Wiltshire

A CIP catalogue record for this book
is available from the British Library

My grateful thanks to Michael Atkinson, Gary Cox, Paul Davidson and Chris Fogg for all their expert help and advice with technical details.

June Thomson

1

Noel Fielding drove his MG with studied nonchalance, one elbow resting on the edge of the open window as, deliberately braking at the last moment, he took the corners of the narrow roads which led to Cressetts.

He was, Roz decided, showing off like a small boy on a bicycle.

Look, everyone! No hands!

She thought she could guess the reason. She had, after all, known him for long enough, ever since their student days together at Bristol University, to recognize the signs. He had always needed her as a witness to any triumph of his, as if she served as a mirror to his success which, without her to reflect it, would not seem quite real even to him.

It was usually a new girl friend. Over the years, she had been introduced to a whole procession of them, none of whom had lasted for more than a few months. Then, after yet another rejection, there would be a gap while he retired to lick his wounds before her phone would ring and he would bounce back into her life with an invitation to dinner or to a party where she would be introduced to the next one.

Roz, I'd like you to meet Sue. Or Flora. Or Sophy.

It was the price she had to pay for never having slept with him. Had she done so, she might have passed into oblivion long ago like all the others. Instead, she had assumed the role of surrogate sister; someone he could confide in; Roz the rock.

And, like a sister, she teased him sometimes; not that he

always noticed. He was almost entirely lacking in any sense of irony.

On this particular occasion, she supposed she had been invited along to act as his audience for another quite different triumph – his part in the G. B. Russell Centenary Festival; an apt simile, as the highlight of the following day's activities was to be a play which Noel was producing and for which she had been roped in as ASM and general dogsbody backstage.

'G. B. Russell?' she had asked, pretending ignorance when Noel had first suggested it. 'Who's he?'

In fact, the name was familiar to her although she hadn't at the time read any of his books.

He was, Noel had explained at some length over the phone, shocked at her apparent lack of knowledge, the detective-fiction writer of the 1920s and 1930s, frightfully well known. He was surprised she hadn't heard of him. Russell was a household name.

'Like Hoover?' she had suggested and when he hadn't got the point, thinking she was referring to J. Edgar, she had added helpfully, 'Or Persil?'

He had laughed dutifully but briefly before adding, 'Seriously though, Roz. . . . '

Seriously though.

It was one of his favourite lines.

The G. B. Russell Festival was, she gathered, a new venture, organized by Oliver Hampden, Russell's grandson and Noel's boss. It was to be held at Cressetts, the family home in Essex, to celebrate the author's birth a hundred years ago on 24 July. About thirty members of the Russell fan society, 'The Cameron Club', would be coming.

'Named after Russell's private detective, Alexander Cameron, of course,' Noel had explained.

'That follows,' Roz had replied, putting her feet up on the sofa and preparing for a long session.

In the past, Noel had explained, the club's activities had consisted solely of a quarterly magazine, produced by someone called Mary Hogarth and distributed by post to the members, known collectively as the 'Cameronians'. But since

8

the successful television series the previous year based on Russell's novels, which had been popular on both sides of the Atlantic, and especially with the centenary of Russell's birth falling that summer, Oliver Hampden had decided to hold a special day-long event, starting off with a short memorial service at his grandfather's grave in Tilney churchyard on the Saturday morning and culminating with a stage adaptation that evening of one of Russell's best-known novels, *The Ingsby Inheritance*.

Which was where Noel came in and, ultimately, Roz herself.

Noel worked as an assistant for Hampden and Brownlow, a public relations organization of which Oliver Hampden was joint managing director, and the previous Christmas had arranged a cabaret for the firm's annual party at the Dorchester, one of Noel's few successes which Roz hadn't personally witnessed. As each employee was allowed only one guest, and as Noel at the time had been heavily involved, it was Lisa who had been invited instead. Or was it Gaynor?

Roz had forgotten.

Anyway, to cut Noel's account down to its essentials, Oliver Hampden had seen the cabaret, had liked it and had asked Noel to adapt *The Ingsby Inheritance* into a play and produce it at Cressetts as part of the G. B. Russell Festival.

Would Roz like to come along and act as Assistant Stage Manager?

As Noel had pointed out, she had plenty of experience, having been, like him, a member of Dramsoc, the student drama society at Bristol University which was where she had in fact first met him. He could promise her a super weekend. Cressetts was beautiful. There'd be plenty of food and champagne. Oliver, and Roz noted with amusement the first-name terms, was charming.

'How many performances?' she had asked cagily.

'Only the one, on Saturday evening,' Noel had assured her. 'It won't last longer than an hour and a half. Oh, do say you'll come, Roz. It won't be difficult. Although I've got a part in the play, I'll be around to give you any help you'll need.'

'Thank you, Noel,' Roz had said, straight-faced. 'That's a great relief.'

The sarcasm was wasted on him.

'So you'll come?'

Well, why not?

Almost anything would be a change from teaching English to foreign students.

So here she was, sitting beside Noel in his MG with the hood down, rollicking through the Essex countryside which looked a damned sight more beautiful than Earls Court, where the Rushdene College for Overseas Studies was situated and where she had her tiny flat.

All those trees! And the scent of grass!

'Smell it!' she shouted to Noel above the rush of the wind.

'Smell what?'

'The country, you idiot. Leaves! Earth!'

He swivelled his head in her direction, wrinkling up his nose as if all the aroma were on her side of the car only.

He still had a young face which, as a student, had been ridiculously adolescent and which now, at twenty-six, the same age as Roz, had preserved that immature, fair-skinned, quality. When he smiled, which he did a lot, boyishly enthusiastic, he was good-looking. But in moments of tension or anxiety, the features seemed to age suddenly, as if the underlying structure had collapsed, revealing unexpected lines and pouches in the flesh.

He looked worried now as he asked, 'You didn't forget your dress for the supper after the play?'

'It's in my suitcase,' she said.

It seemed there was to be a buffet party on Saturday evening at which everyone was expected to wear 1920s dress, the period in which the play was set. Roz had hired hers, a black sequinned affair with a low–cut waist and knee-length skirt, and rather fancied herself in it. Being small and thin and dark, she flattered herself that she looked like a *femme fatale* from a Hollywood silent movie – Louise Brooks or Pola Negri.

And then Noel added, double-declutching extravagantly as

they roared into another S-bend, 'Annabel's keen on getting everything exactly right.'

Annabel.

There was a special note in his voice as he spoke the name and Roz thought, Oh, God, here we go again!

'Who's Annabel?' she asked, trying not to sound either too interested or too exasperated.

'Didn't I tell you about her?'

'No, you didn't.'

'Well, she's someone I met at a party a couple of months ago. She does a fashion column for *Rave*, that new women's mag. Annabel Thorpe. You've heard of her?'

'I only ever read *Vogue*,' Roz told him with apparent seriousness.

She needn't have bothered. Noel was oblivious.

'Anyway, we got talking about the play and she seemed interested so I said would she like to do the costumes, because Oliver's given me an absolutely free hand with the production, and she said she'd love to. You'll meet her at Cressetts. She came down earlier today. Actually, I've given her a part in the play – Lady Ingsby – and she's terrific. A natural. I've been seeing quite a lot of her lately as a matter of fact, rehearsing and so on, either at her flat or mine.'

But the 'so on' couldn't have been all that serious, Roz thought. If Noel and Annabel were lovers, Roz would have heard of her. Noel would have been on the phone long ago.

So Annabel was proving elusive.

She also wondered if the invitation to Cressetts was to witness a double triumph, not just the play but Noel's final conquest of Annabel.

Out loud, she said, 'What's she like? Attractive?'

'Attractive? She's gorgeous. Cool. Blonde. You know the type?' He gave her an oblique glance to gauge her reaction as he added, 'Actually, she's the daughter of Bernard Thorpe, you know, the City financier.'

'Gosh! You are moving in high circles these days,' Roz remarked. 'Oliver Hampden and now the daughter of Bernard Thorpe!'

11

She saw him smile to himself, the corners of his mouth flickering upwards with an expression of self-congratulation, and as they roared into another bend in the road she thought with amused exasperation how transparent he was. Oddly enough, it was one of the reasons she liked him. Unlike other men she'd known, with Noel she didn't have to dig about to find his ego. It was instantly obvious. That was part of his charm.

The road descended a hill with a wood on the left and open farmland on the right. As the car tore past she caught a glimpse of barley bristling in the sun. It looked crisp and bleached; almost ready for harvesting.

At the bottom lay the village of Tilney, smaller than Roz had expected. A few houses; a pub; a shop; the whole place dominated by the flint tower of a church, half-hidden in its surrounding trees.

A broad gravelled drive lined with beeches ran alongside the church, leading, Roz assumed, to the rectory.

To her surprise, Noel slowed down and turned into it, driving with exaggerated care after the dash and speed of the rest of the journey towards a pair of tall wrought-iron gates which stood open at the far end.

'Cressetts,' Noel announced proudly, as if the place belonged to him. 'Don't you think it's beautiful?'

They had entered a large, cobble-stoned courtyard, enclosed on one side by a high wall with an arched opening in it, on the other two by the bays of the house which formed an L-shape.

Both wall and house were built of ancient, narrow bricks, rosy-pink in the afternoon sun, swagged in places by old-fashioned climbing roses, loose-petalled and scented. As she got out of the car, Roz could smell their heavy fragrance.

The structure of the house was extraordinary, its outline broken by stepped gables and small towers which rose at unexpected corners. Here and there oriel windows jutted out from the upper storeys while on the ground floor more window bays thrust themselves out, surmounted with their own crenellated parapets.

12

The steep roof, which was covered with tiles the same colour as the bricks, followed a similar irregular and complex pattern, its slopes broken by small triangular attic dormers or the bases to clusters of tall chimney stacks, some twisted into barley-sugar shapes, others decorated with zigzag or chequer-board patterns, and all of them topped with elaborate terra-cotta crowns.

It was not only beautiful; it was eccentric, bewitching, ut-terly delightful.

The front door faced them, set in its own battlemented bay. Carrying her suitcase, Roz followed Noel into a large, flagged hall, furnished with an Elizabethan court cupboard and two high-backed, carved chairs of the same period.

Several doors led off the hall but all were closed and the house seemed deserted.

'Where is everybody?' Noel asked in an aggrieved voice, dumping his suitcase down. He seemed piqued that no one was there to welcome them.

As if in answer to his question, a door on the right opened and a woman came forward to greet them.

She was tall and, at first sight, strikingly attractive, with a great quantity of dark hair which sprang in heavy tendrils about her head, giving the impression of a Spanish gypsy. Her clothes, a loose black dress of Indian cotton which reached down to her calves, the hem and neckline embroidered with a broad band of red and yellow flowers, emphasized this quality of southern richness.

It was only when she approached them that Roz was aware of a tension about her which was altogether English, apparent in the set of her shoulders and the awkward manner in which she held out her hand in greeting.

But that face! It was both beautiful and tragic.

Although the bone structure was classic, it was too close to the surface of the skin which was stretched so tight that one was uncomfortably aware of the skull below the flesh, the high prominences of the forehead and the cheekbones, and par-ticularly the hollows of the eyes in which the eyes themselves,

13

huge and brilliant, seemed to have been burnt into the sockets.

Roz was reminded of the ruin of some once-noble cathedral or abbey, where the softening layer of plaster and decoration had fallen away, revealing the stark skeleton of the underlying architecture.

Noel made the introductions in a perfunctory manner, still put out, it appeared, that their arrival had excited no other interest.

'Mary Hogarth, Roz Bennet,' adding before the two women had finished shaking hands, 'where are the others?'

'Annabel's gone into Widford to do some shopping and Oliver's on the phone to the caterers,' Mary Hogarth replied. 'He asked me to show you up to your rooms. We're all to meet in about half an hour in the drawing-room for tea.'

She began to lead the way up a broad oak staircase, its shallow uncarpeted treads worn hollow in the centre by centuries of feet.

At the top, it opened on to a wide landing furnished like a small sitting-room with a winged armchair covered in faded tapestry and a glass-fronted cabinet full of Dresden china.

Here Mary Hogarth turned to the right along a passage, low-ceilinged and heavily beamed like a gallery on an old timber-framed ship, its uneven floor of polished boards giving the impression that the whole structure was lifting and falling with some gentle, unseen swell.

In places, a small, cock-eyed window gave unexpected glimpses not of the sea but of a garden or the courtyard, sudden slanting views of walls, lawns, herbaceous borders.

The gallery ran in the same haphazard fashion, turning sharply to left or right, ascending or descending to different levels by means of shallow steps, until it finally broadened out into an inner hall.

It was here that Mary Hogarth paused and began opening doors.

The first revealed a narrow, twisting staircase, set into the width of the wall.

'It leads directly down to the drawing-room,' Mary Hogarth

explained. 'It's quicker than using the main stairs.' Throwing open another door, she added, 'Oliver's put you in here, Noel.'

'Oh, the green room.' Noel seemed put out. 'Who am I sharing a bathroom with?'

'Christie.'

'And where's Annabel sleeping then?'

'In the other wing.'

'Is she?' Noel sounded surprised and disappointed as if he'd counted on Annabel's room being next to his. 'In that case,' he continued, 'I suppose Roz gets the blue. You're honoured, Roz. It's the nicest of the guest bedrooms. Lovely view and your own bath. Lucky you.'

He disappeared inside his own room, leaving Mary Hogarth to conduct Roz to hers.

It was a pretty room, hung with sprigged wallpaper which matched the curtains at the casement windows and at the head of a half-tester bed. The furniture was antique but lighter and more delicate than the heavier Tudor pieces in the hall downstairs: a small rosewood table with a shield-shaped mirror standing on its top which served as a dressing-table; a low, button-backed chair; a tall bow-fronted chest of drawers.

After the approach to it along the low-ceilinged passage, the room was larger and brighter than Roz had expected. When she commented on this, Mary Hogarth said, 'It's in the newer part of the house.'

'Newer?'

'Well, Carolean, 1665. Bits were added on at different periods. The oldest part is early Tudor, including the Stone Gallery where the party will be held. Then there's the Elizabethan wing where G.B.'s study is and the family bedrooms. I expect Oliver will show you over the place after supper, if there's time.'

She seemed ill at ease yet loath to leave, poised between a need for intimacy and a desire for flight. And all the time she was speaking, Roz noticed her hands kept touching objects in the room with an uncertain but lingering caress, moving a

15

silver candlestick on the dressing-table or smoothing down a faded patchwork counterpane which covered the bed.

Roz said brightly, 'Noel tells me you run a bookshop in Widford.'

It was not the right approach. Mary Hogarth drew back, her hands suddenly still.

'Yes,' was all she said.

Then what intimacy was she looking for, if not to talk about herself? Roz wondered.

Turning towards the window, she tried again. 'I love the view.'

It was indeed beautiful. The window overlooked a broad, flag-stoned terrace and a long sweep of lawn which led down to an ornamental pool surrounded by a low brick wall with a curved coping. In the centre of the pool rose the bronze figure of a naked girl. She was stretching upwards on tiptoe, arms held high, head flung back as if in some silent and private ecstasy which the observer had come upon only by chance.

'That's where the second scene in the play will be held; you know, the one in the garden,' Mary Hogarth said. 'There'll be lights in the trees and the pool will be floodlit. It should look spectacular. Oliver wanted to make use of the garden.'

It was the second time she had used his name and Roz was aware that on each occasion Mary Hogarth had deliberately manipulated the conversation in order to include it.

So he was the reason behind Mary Hogarth's need for intimacy. She had to talk about him, feel his name in her mouth, in much the same way as she felt compelled to touch the objects in the room as part of the material substance of his background.

It was obsessive and also disturbing.

As if aware that she had given too much away, Mary Hogarth moved across the room.

'The bathroom's through there,' she said, indicating a door. 'It's very small, I'm afraid, but at least you won't have to share. Tea will be in about half an hour. Come down when you're ready, Miss Bennet.'

'Oh, Roz, please,' Roz protested.

16

But the door had already closed and Roz doubted if Mary Hogarth had heard her.

Left alone, Roz unpacked before showering and changing into a dress. Tea in the drawing-room sounded formal, not the occasion for jeans and a T-shirt.

She was sitting on the bed, taking a quick look at the script to remind herself of the action of the play, when Noel knocked perfunctorily before sticking his head round the door.

'Are you decent?'

He had changed, too, into dark blue linen slacks and a blue and white striped shirt, the sleeves of which were rolled up to show he meant to get down to business. A blue silk cravat, knotted carelessly in the open neck of his shirt, added a more dilettante touch, the actor-producer with artistic pretensions.

'I think we ought to go down,' he went on, sounding fussed. 'We don't want to keep Oliver waiting.'

That name again! As if Oliver Hampden was the only damn person who mattered!

Roz folded the script up crossly. Even before she had met the man, she had begun to dislike him.

'And bring the script with you,' Noel continued. 'I want to do a walk-through with you after tea.'

'All right. I was going to anyway,' Roz retorted.

Shoving it under her arm, she stalked over to the door, following Noel down the narrow staircase to a lower hall and from there into a large panelled drawing-room with a heavily embossed ceiling, all plaster fruit and flowers, and three long windows which looked out over the garden.

The room was intimidatingly full of people. As Roz might have guessed it was Oliver Hampden who first made his presence known, coming forward, hand already extended, to introduce himself with a practised ease.

If she had not already been put on her guard, first by Noel's and then by Mary Hogarth's too obvious admiration, she might have been taken in by him.

Oliver Hampden was certainly attractive: older than she had expected; in his early forties; distinguished-looking with touches of grey in his dark hair. But more than his physical presence, he gave off a strong aura of self-assurance and power which, under other circumstances, she would have found disturbing.

As it was, she was looking for a flaw and she found it.

He was a smoothie, she decided, who had an eye fixed on the main chance whether sexual or financial; clever but not to be trusted and too accustomed to using his charm to get his own way.

At the same time she was aware, as he took her hand in his, enfolding it in a warm intimacy, that he had already summed her up and dismissed her as too small and not pretty enough.

It amused rather than offended her. At least, she thought wryly, I shan't have to spend the weekend avoiding his advances.

'Miss Bennet – Roz, may I? – it was delightful of you to agree to come,' he was saying, steering her across the room. 'You must meet the others. My mother, Lady Kelling. My younger brother, Christopher, known in the family as Christie. Annabel still hasn't got back from Widford but you'll meet her later. Mary Hogarth, you already know. And our own indispensable Clifford Teague who's in charge of the sound and lighting effects for the play.'

It was a series of carefully graded introductions, starting at the top and working down, Clifford Teague, who was presumably the least socially important, receiving the longest accolade.

Roz made the rounds, shaking hands and exchanging short pleasantries before finally retiring to a chair by one of the long windows with a cup of tea and a plate containing a slice of Victoria sponge cake, dispensed by Mary Hogarth who was in charge of the trolley. She sat for a few moments in silence to consolidate her first impressions of these strangers.

First Lady Kelling.

In the course of several long conversations with Noel either over the phone or during meetings to discuss the play at various pubs and restaurants, she had learned enough about the Hampden family to know that Lady Kelling was the only child of G. B. Russell and had been married first to Oliver and

18

Christie's father, John Hampden, who had owned an unsuccessful literary magazine before the war, then to Lord Kelling, the industrialist, created a life peer by the post-war Attlee government. Widowed twice, she now lived at Cressetts, acting as hostess for Oliver, a bachelor, who as the oldest grandson had inherited the house under the terms of his grandfather's will.

Oliver had inherited something else besides bricks and mortar: his mother's sharpness of mind and sense of presence, although in her case the shrewdness was more evident, less disguised by charm and ease of manners.

She was a formidable old lady who would not suffer fools gladly. It was apparent in her upright carriage and the direct expression in her eyes, surprisingly young and bright under a coronet of white hair. There was an aloofness about her which Roz had been aware of as they shook hands, despite the smile and the cordiality of her welcome.

I shall reserve my judgement of you for the time being, that clasp had suggested.

Roz had been too put out by this response, following so quickly on Oliver's dismissal of her as unbedworthy, to take in much of Christie, the younger brother, apart from a brief impression of a man in his thirties, thinner and untidier in appearance than Oliver Hampden, more angular in the features and lacking much of his brother's surface gloss although he shared with the rest of the family that look of bright-eyed intelligence. There had been an air of amused irreverence about him which she rather liked.

From what Noel had told her about him, she knew he was married with two sons aged eleven and thirteen. His wife lectured in art history while he ran a small publishing firm which specialized in children's books.

He was to take the part in the play of Alexander Cameron, G. B. Russell's private detective, a role which, having now met him, Roz thought would suit him.

Physically he was a good match. Cameron was described as dark-haired, lean-faced, keen-eyed. And Christie had the right presence as well – that Hampden quality of social ease

19

which G. B. Russell had apparently also possessed though the son of an Edinburgh draper's assistant, and with which he had endowed his main character. However, Russell, whom Roz suspected of being something of a snob, had been at pains to hint that the royal blood of the Stuarts ran in Cameron's veins and to give his character an impeccable upper-class English background including an education at Eton and Oxford, a taste for good claret and an interest in art and music about which he was an acknowledged expert.

Christie Hampden could easily fit that role.

Glancing across the room at him to confirm this impression, she was disconcerted to find he was looking at her. As their glances met, he smiled with an odd intimacy which hinted at some conspiracy between them, about what or against whom she had no idea.

Giving him a brief smile in return which committed her to nothing, Roz turned her attention to the last member of the group to be introduced – Clifford Teague. He was a thin, taciturn man, brown hair already receding to show a high, narrow forehead, although he must have been about the same age as Noel and Roz. He was leaning forward, elbows on knees, his teacup held awkwardly in both hands, listening with an air of frowning intensity to the conversation between Oliver and Noel who, as if to emphasize their roles as impresario and producer, had remained standing in front of the fireplace discussing the play, Oliver relaxed, Noel too tense and eager to explain.

He was saying, 'Were you able to get hold of a second console for the scene by the pool? It'll add tremendously to the dramatic effect if the lights can be gradually brought up as the audience walks across the lawn.'

Oliver turned to Teague. 'That's your department, Cliff.'

Teague said shortly, 'I made one in the end; cheaper than hiring.'

'Made one? Good Lord, really? That's incredible!'

Teague seemed to take offence at Noel's surprise. Roz saw him scowl and the muscles in his neck stiffen.

It was Oliver who retrieved the situation by remarking,

'You know Cliff. He can turn his hand to anything. I don't know how I'd run this place without him.'

While the comment was made as a compliment to Teague, it was also a subtle rebuke to Noel who put down his empty cup.

'Yes, well, if that's all organized, perhaps I'd better take Roz on walkabout, introduce her to the sets and so on before this evening's rehearsal. Are you coming, Oliver? I'm sure she would love to look over the house at the same time.'

'I'll leave that to you, Noel,' Oliver replied, glancing at his watch. 'You know the place pretty well by now and I've got several more rather important phone calls to make.'

It was clearly a form of dismissal although the party was already beginning to break up. Lady Kelling had risen to her feet, grasping a silver-knobbed cane in one hand, her other arm in Christie's.

'I shall leave you younger people to your play,' she announced in a decisive voice which gave Roz the impression she didn't entirely approve of the arrangements for the Russell Festival.

Cliff Teague had already slipped quietly away through one of the sets of long windows into the garden which left Mary Hogarth, who seemed to be acting as domestic help, to collect the used plates and cups.

To show solidarity with her, Roz carried her own tea things over to the trolley.

She had begun to feel a little exasperated by the situation; not for her own sake but for Mary Hogarth's and Noel's, although part of her anger was also directed at them.

Weren't they aware they were being used? Or were they too blinded by Oliver's charm and his mother's dominant role in the household to see it?

She would make damn sure that no one in the family, certainly not Oliver Hampden, was going to manipulate her in the same manner.

2

To Roz's relief, Noel appeared not to have noticed Oliver's dismissal of him. As soon as they left the drawing-room, he enthusiastically threw himself into the role of guide, directing her along a passage which, like the corridor upstairs, twisted and turned as it followed the eccentric layout of the house.

From time to time, he stopped to open doors, the first to G. B. Russell's study. As Mary Hogarth had explained, it was in the Elizabethan part of the house and the room with its low, beamed ceiling and panelled walls had the brooding and curiously static air of a place set aside more as a museum than part of a family home.

There was the great man's desk standing in front of the window, with his pentray and notebooks laid out on its surface, his collection of pipes in a wooden rack at hand, while his broad-brimmed hat and plaid cloak, the clothes with which he was associated and in which he had so often been photographed, were hanging on an old-fashioned bentwood coat-stand, as if Russell's ghost still inhabited the room.

The walls were hung with some of these photographs – G.B. with H. G. Wells, G.B. with friends at Ascot or on some millionaire's yacht at Cannes – while a portrait of G.B. by Sir James Gunn, alone and attired in the plaid cloak, was displayed above the stone fireplace, fixing the visitor with a keen blue gaze and looking so disconcertingly like his grandson, Oliver Hampden, with that same charming half-smile and air of well-nourished *bonhomie*, that Roz was relieved when Noel shut the door on him and they continued the tour, crossing a

22

small inner vestibule with a glazed door which led on to the terrace.

'That's a quick way into the garden,' Noel remarked. 'There's also a downstairs loo there as well.'

Here the corridor made a sharp left turn towards the main entrance hall and as they walked along it, passing another closed door, Noel added, 'And that's Lady Kelling's private sitting-room. I'd better not show you that. She uses it a lot when Oliver brings guests down to Cressetts.'

The next door led into the dining-room, emptied for the occasion of the play of all its normal furniture which had been replaced by rows of gilt chairs facing a low dais at the far end, already set for the first and third acts of *The Ingsby Inheritance*.

Roz could see now what Noel had meant about the problems of staging the play although, when he had gone on and on about them over the phone, she had thought it was just Noel making a fuss.

It was a long, narrow room and, like the drawing-room, had three sets of curtained doors, Gothic in style, which opened on to the terrace. In order to incorporate one of these pairs of doors into the set for use as an entrance and exit, it had been necessary to bring the stage well forward, creating an awkwardly shaped acting area, longer from front to back than it was wide. This in turn had limited the space in what normally would have been the wings.

On the prompt side it wasn't too bad. There was room for her to sit and still be hidden from the audience by the front-of-house tabs. It was on the OP side that the problems arose. Here the curtain wasn't wide enough to conceal the table on which Cliff Teague's lighting and sound consoles had been set up or the portable lighting stands; they were masked from view by a folding screen.

As for the rest of the set, Noel had done his best with these unsatisfactory conditions, keeping the props to a minimum. A high-backed chair, a desk on which stood an old-fashioned telephone, and a bookcase full of leather-bound volumes surmounted by a marble bust of Plato were enough to suggest the library at Highwood House.

Stage right, the pair of doors was supposed to lead into the hall of Highwood House and a piece of scenery, covered with wallpaper and with a painting hanging on it, had been propped up at an angle just outside the doors to hide the view of the terrace and the garden.

An overhead gantry carrying the fixed lamp battens at the front of the stage was already in place; so, too, was a tubular metal frame on which were suspended the tabs and the proscenium border.

Noel strode down the length of the room, invigorated and very much in charge.

'OK! OK!' he was saying. 'Let me put you in the picture, Roz. Scene one. You'll be in charge of the front-of-house tabs as well as acting as prompt. Oliver will already be on the set with the tabs closed before the audience comes in. Wyvern, one of the chaps I've roped in from the Widford Players who's taking the part of the butler, will conduct them to their seats. As they arrive, Cliff'll be playing the tape of Coward's "Lady Be Good". As soon as the audience is settled and Wyvern's dimmed the house lights you'll have to give Cliff the nod, because he can't see the main part of the room from behind that screen. He'll then fade out the music and bring up the lights on the set. As soon as they start to go up, it's your job to open the tabs from the prompt side.'

He rustled about behind them.

'Damn! I asked Mary to put a chair out for you but she's obviously forgotten. It's always the same; better to do things yourself than rely on anybody else.'

'I'll get a chair,' Roz said. It seemed to her that Mary Hogarth already had enough to do. 'Go on. What else in act one?'

'There's not much more. As you know, there's the phone call half-way through from Tranter, the American art dealer. . . . ' He broke off to exclaim dramatically, clutching at his temples. 'Oh my God!'

'What's the matter?' Roz demanded.

'Frank Clayton, the man who plays Tranter. He rang me this morning. He won't be able to make it for the supper Oliver's laying on this evening for the cast. I should have mentioned it to Oliver over tea.'

'But he'll be there surely for the rehearsal?' Roz asked.

'Oh, heavens, yes. At least, I hope to God he is. If he drops out as well. . . . ' He broke off, looking harassed.

Roz patted his arm comfortingly. 'It can't happen twice,' she said.

The problem of the actor who was to play Tranter had arisen the previous week and had been the subject of an anguished and interminable telephone call from Noel which had taken up the best part of an evening. The original actor had been forced to give up the part when his wife was taken to hospital with a heart attack. Arnold Wyvern, from the Widford Players, had found a last-minute replacement, Frank Clayton, who had agreed to take over the role; not as good as Maitland, the original actor, but passable, according to Noel who had rushed down to Widford to rehearse him. At least he knew the lines and the costume fitted.

'We'll have to see how Clayton makes out at tonight's rehearsal,' Noel was saying. 'Seriously though, Roz, I sometimes wish I hadn't taken on the damn play in the first place. It's taken up a hell of a lot of time. I only agreed because Oliver asked me personally.'

He ran a hand through his hair and Roz realized that underneath his apparent confidence he was deeply concerned about the play's success.

'Let's hope Oliver is suitably grateful,' she observed tartly.

'Oh, he is; he is,' Noel assured her. 'I'm quite sure of that. I'll have to have a word with him later about Clayton. Anyway,' and he took a deep breath and flexed his shoulders, Noel's way of trying to relax in moments of tension, 'to get back to scene one. Cliff should have set it up for the phone to ring. I'll check with him later that he's done it. The whole scene only lasts about twenty minutes. On Annabel's exit line, "Oh, Philip, can't we even talk these days without arguing?", Cliff will start a slow lighting fade and as Oliver sits down at the desk with his head in his hands, you'll draw the tabs. But I want a slow close; don't rush it.'

25

Roz nodded and marked it in her script as Noel continued, 'As soon as the tabs are closed, Wyvern will turn on the main lights and start getting the audience out by the door at the back, across the hall and round to the pool. While they're exiting, Cliff will have faded in the music – "Some Day I'll Find You" this time, a bit more sombre to set the mood. Then, once the room is cleared, he'll cut the lights and sound and nip out by the doors in the set and across the terrace to take over the effects for the outdoor scene. He'll have plenty of time. There'll be about thirty in the audience and it'll take several minutes to get them all out and into the garden.'

'Supposing it rains?' Roz asked.

It seemed to her a reasonable enough question but Noel took it personally.

'It isn't going to bloody rain! I checked the long-range weather forecast and it said warm, dry and settled. Oliver's taken out insurance against it raining.'

He would, Roz thought. Out loud she persisted, 'But if it does?'

'Then the scene'll have to be played in the entrance hall with a couple of tubs of flowers and a bench to suggest the garden setting. It won't be the same, though, as having it by the pool. Anyhow, we'll worry about that tomorrow, if it rains. Which it won't. And now can we get on?' he asked in a harassed voice. 'There's still loads to run through.'

Leading the way out of the dining-room, he turned out of the passage into the main hall where he and Roz had first been met by Mary Hogarth on their arrival.

'OK. The audience will exit through the front door, walk across the courtyard and through the archway into the garden. As soon as they've left, you'll take over in here.' He flung open a door to the right of the hall which led into a beamed and panelled room, part sitting-room, part office, furnished with club armchairs upholstered in leather, and a large, heavily carved oak desk on which a fax machine, two modern telephones, an IBM computer and a photocopier looked oddly out of keeping with the surroundings.

'It's Oliver's private den,' Noel explained. 'I've bagged it because it's the only room on the ground floor where you can get a good view of the pool.'

He indicated the window through which Roz could indeed glimpse a vista similar to the one from her own bedroom, of the lawn sloping gently down towards the ornamental pool with its attendant nymph.

'You'll have to keep a watch on the action from here,' Noel explained, 'because it'll be your job to fire the prop gun through the window at the right moment. I've had to arrange it like this because you can't see the set properly from the dining-room; there's too many bushes in the way. The cue'll be after Annabel makes her exit and walks to the bottom of the terrace steps. As soon as you've done that, you go back to the dining-room to arrange the set. By then, Oliver will have changed into the shirt with the bloodstains on the front and should be ready to take up his position, lying back in the chair. And for God's sake don't forget to take the gun with you. You put it down on the floor by his right hand. *Right* hand, remember. It's the clue that he's been murdered. The pen and inkwell are on his left on the desk. You'd better check that they are before tomorrow night's performance. I wouldn't put it past some damned fool to move them. Once you've arranged the gun and scattered the blackmail letters on the floor, you take your place behind the tabs ready to open them once the audience is back in place. Annabel and some of the others will come on set through the garden doors, including Cliff who'll do the light and sound for the next two scenes.'

'Who'll prompt for the scene by the pool?' Roz asked.

'No one. There isn't anyone to spare. Anyway it's only Annabel and me – our big love scene,' Noel said, grinning in anticipation, 'and I'm damned sure I know my part. Let's hope Annabel remembers hers. We'll find that out this evening at rehearsal. Wyvern as butler only comes on at the end of the scene with just a few lines and he's reliable. Anything else you need to know?'

'I don't think so. It doesn't sound too difficult.'

'Don't you believe it,' Noel said. He seemed plunged into sudden gloom. 'It's a hell of a lot more complicated than you

27

think and with only the one proper rehearsal, anything could go wrong. We had a couple of run-throughs at Cressetts a fortnight ago but not with the sets and effects. We'll have to see how it goes tonight. Well, while we're here, let's take a look at the Stone Gallery and then I want to have a quick check on the set-up in the garden.'

They crossed the entrance hall to a pair of double doors on the far side which Noel opened with a flourish, anticipating Roz's reaction with the remark, 'Rather splendid, isn't it?'

I wish, Roz thought with a little burst of exasperation, that he'd stop doing that. I don't need him to tell me what to think.

'Part of the original early Tudor manor house,' he added, also unnecessarily. Roz could see that for herself.

It was large and very stark, the floor paved with worn flag-stones. The walls, also of stone, were hung with two large faded tapestries of hunting scenes; above was a heavily raftered ceiling, the end bosses of which were carved in the shape of boars' heads.

Given the weight of stone and timber, it should have been oppressive but at one end a large window, arched and mullioned like the east window of a church and inset with panels depicting heraldic coats of arms, let in the sunlight which fell in a dazzling oblong across the floor, spattered with blobs and lozenges of azure, topaz and crimson, reflected down through the stained glass.

Facing the window at the opposite end of the room and acting as a foil to its airy brightness was a vast stone chimney-breast with a massive fireplace which occupied the whole wall.

In front of it Mary Hogarth was kneeling on the floor. On a white sheet spread out beside her lay armfuls of flowers, roses, delphiniums and tall spikes of white and orange lilies, which she was arranging in a large copper urn that stood on the hearth.

She looked, Roz thought, like a woman at prayer as she knelt there, nunlike in her long black dress, her head submissively bowed, and so totally absorbed in her task that she was unaware of their presence in the doorway.

Two men, presumably from the caterers', were setting up a long buffet table against the far wall for the party the following evening. Small round tables, not yet covered with cloths and with their accompanying chairs up-ended on top of them, had already been arranged along the sides of the room.

Noel closed the door on them.

'What's the gallery used for?' Roz asked as they let themselves out by the front door and crossed the courtyard towards the garden. She could not imagine the family sitting there in the evenings. Despite its spendour, it was hardly cosy.

'Oliver uses it for conferences and receptions for people he brings down from London and wants to impress. They usually are – impressed, I mean, especially the Americans and the Japanese. English heritage and all that. In G.B.'s time, it was used for family parties, especially charades at Christmas. It would've been perfect, of course, for staging the play but Oliver needed it for the buffet afterwards. Evidently old G.B. was very keen on amateur dramatics; that was one of the reasons why Oliver wanted to put on a play for the centenary.'

'Family heritage and all that?' Roz suggested.

He gave her a sideways glance, not sure if she was pulling his leg. 'Seriously though, Roz, tradition's important; a sense of history; a feeling for the past. Someone's got to keep it going.'

Roz began to laugh and then, seeing his pained expression, put an arm companionably in his. 'I've got nothing against the past, providing it isn't taken too far. I can't say I'm keen on Elizabethan banquets with serving wenches and men in tights playing sackbuts.'

'But it's a huge business, the past!' Noel protested. 'I don't know how much it adds to the GNP but it must be a hefty slice.'

'And Oliver? How much will he make out of the Russell Festival?'

Noel looked shocked. 'I don't think he's thought of it like that.'

'Hasn't he? You surprise me. I shouldn't imagine he does anything without working out the profit and loss first. Or is he

29

in it for the prestige? I can't see him making much money on it unless he's planning to write the loss off against tax.'

'You don't like him much,' Noel said. It was almost an accusation.

'Not a lot,' Roz agreed cheerfully.

She could have said more but decided against it. Noel had enough on his plate without her adding to his problems by criticizing Oliver Hampden to him. After all, the man was Noel's boss and it was Noel who had to deal with him on a day-to-day basis.

While they were speaking, they had crossed the courtyard, passing through the archway, and had entered the main garden which lay behind the house. The terrace and the glazed doors which opened off the dining-room and gave the actors access to the garden lay over to their far right. Ahead of them, the long gentle slope of the lawn led down towards the ornamental pool where Cliff Teague could be seen at work, unrolling coils of electric cable.

He broke off from the task as they approached and stood waiting, scowling into the sun.

Faced with a practical concern regarding the play, Noel immediately recovered his spirits.

'Where's the other console going, Cliff?' he asked.

'Over there.' Teague jerked a thumb in the direction of a clump of rhododendron bushes which lay to the right of the pool.

'Fine! Fine! A good spot!' Noel exclaimed approvingly. 'I assume it can't be seen by the audience? Right! Let's have a look at it then. It's the one you made yourself, isn't it?'

As the two of them walked away discussing the lighting, Roz sat down on the stone coping which surrounded the pool and watched their backs speculatively. Noel was gesticulating enthusiastically while Teague remained silent, his hands stuffed in the pockets of his jeans. There was a defensive look about the set of his shoulders as if he resented Noel's interference.

Roz wondered about Cliff Teague. Noel had told her very little about him, referring to him merely as the person in charge of the sound and lighting effects for the play. She had no idea what place, if any, he occupied in the household or what his relationship was with Oliver Hampden.

It was a question she put to Noel when, having emerged from the shrubbery, brushing loose pieces of dead leaf from his trousers, he joined her at the pool.

'Cliff?' he said. 'Didn't I tell you? He lives here.'

'Here? At Cressetts, you mean?'

'Well, not exactly in the main house. Oliver's given him a small flat over one of the old stables. The downstairs part's been converted into a workshop for him. He's a sort of handyman round the place; does maintenance work, a bit of gardening and chauffeuring; looks after the cars. Actually, he's good. He can turn his hand to almost anything. He's made a damned good job of putting together that second console.'

'Is he married?'

'Not that I know of.' He grinned at her slyly. 'Why? You don't fancy him, do you?'

'No, you fool. I'm just curious.'

She left it there, not wanting to explain that she found Cliff Teague interesting; more complex than she had thought when she was first introduced to him. There was a closed-in, brooding quality about him which she found more intriguing than Oliver Hampden's easy charm.

Changing the subject, she went on, 'Tell me more about Mary Hogarth.'

That was another person about whom she was curious.

Noel shifted about uneasily beside her on the coping. An uncomplicated man himself, he was never comfortable discussing other people's personalities.

'I think I've told you all I know. She runs a bookshop in Widford; I think she was divorced years ago; anyway, there's no husband or children; and she edits the magazine for the Russell fan club.'

'Why?'

'What do you mean, why? Because she wants to, I suppose.'

'Not because of Oliver?'

31

Noel's reply came a little too quickly and sharply. 'What are you getting at?'

·'I wondered if she's in love with him.'

'God, you're nosy, Roz! If she is, it's nothing to do with us. Oliver certainly isn't in love with her.' He broke off with evident relief as the figure of a woman appeared on the terrace, waved at them and began descending the steps. 'Oh, good! Here's Annabel. At last!'

Getting to his feet, he began loping up the lawn towards her, arms already spread wide in a theatrical gesture of greeting.

From her vantage point beside the pool, Roz was able to observe their meeting.

It was significant, she thought, that just before Noel reached her, Annabel put on a pair of large-lensed sun-glasses which, up to that moment, she had been carrying in her hand. The gesture was defensive, designed to keep him at arm's length. So, too, was the manner in which she avoided his lips, offering only her cheek for him to kiss.

In his delight at seeing her, Noel seemed unaware of any coolness in her manner as, beaming broadly, he took her by the elbow and conducted her ceremoniously down the lawn to where Roz was sitting.

'Roz, I'd like you to meet Annabel. Annabel, Roz.'

The two women smiled and nodded in greeting, Annabel remaining standing despite Noel's attempts to persuade her to join them.

'I can't stop, Noel. I've only just got back from Widford which was ghastly; crowds of people. And the heat! I feel totally shattered. I must shower and change.'

To Roz, she looked anything but shattered. Annabel was one of those women who manage to remain infuriatingly cool and elegant under any circumstances. Her cream blouse – wild silk, surely? – and a biscuit-coloured linen skirt looked newly ironed; her hair impeccable. It was cut in a short, blonde bob, one gleaming wing falling across her cheek in an artless curve which only the very best West End stylist could have achieved.

32

Was she as gorgeous as Noel had described her?

She was certainly attractive but observing her closely as she stood talking to Noel about the ghastliness of Widford, Roz wasn't so sure.

There was a hardness about the angle of her jaw and a lack of animation in her expression which made her, in Roz's eyes, less interesting than Mary Hogarth.

And one thing was absolutely obvious: she was not nearly as ecstatic about Noel as he was about her.

His face creased up with sympathy, he was leaning forward and listening with rapt attention to her account of her shopping expedition that afternoon – something about trying to buy some velvet ribbon for a headband to match her costume and how she'd had to try five different shops before she'd found it.

And now she really must have a shower and a rest.

She waved briefly to Roz before setting off across the lawn towards the house, Noel escorting her for part of the way until, at her insistence, he left her to continue alone.

For several moments, he remained standing, watching her departure, a forlorn figure, like a small boy who has been dismissed by a much-loved adult.

When he returned, he still looked crestfallen. 'She's tired,' he said.

'I gathered that,' Roz replied.

She would have liked to say more but held her tongue. Annabel, like Oliver Hampden, would have to be treated as a taboo subject as far as Noel was concerned although she longed to warn him.

It's no good, she wanted to say. I don't know what there's been between you but, as far as she's concerned, it's over.

'The trouble is,' Noel continued, anxious to explain and excuse, 'she's such a perfectionist. Everything has to be just right. She's even had her hair done differently.'

'Has she?' It sounded ominous to Roz. 'How was it before?'

'Well, long and sort of crinkly.' He gestured vaguely around his own head, indicating a more extravagant style. 'It suits her, though. Don't you agree, Roz? Don't you think she's fabulous?'

'Oh, utterly,' Roz said quickly. 'She'll be ideal for Lady Ingsby. She has just the right manner. And speaking of the play, shouldn't we finish the run-through?'

'Oh, Lord, yes!' He turned his wrist to look at his watch. 'It's nearly a quarter past six now and supper's at seven, early so there'll be plenty of time for the rehearsal afterwards.'

For the last two scenes which were to take place on the set for the library at Highwood House, they returned to the dining-room, entering from the terrace through the glass doors. There was no sign of Annabel; or of anyone else come to that.

The last part of the play was relatively straightforward. Roz made notes on her script as Noel took her through it: a slow curtain opening on the first of the scenes which would reveal Oliver, as Lord Ingsby, lying slumped back in the chair behind the desk, the starched evening shirt he had worn at the beginning of the play changed for one with bloodstains on the front. Then, after Christie's entrance as Alexander Cameron, Russell's aristocratic private detective, and his examination of the body, there'd be a fast curtain close following immediately after his announcement that it was a case of murder.

It was only at the end of this scene that Roz had anything to do, apart from prompting.

Once the curtains were closed, there was to be a short interval, long enough for Oliver Hampden to leave the stage through the glass doors and for her, as ASM, to gather up the scattered blackmail letters, remove the gun from the floor and place it on the desk. At the same time, Noel and Cliff Teague would carry a couple of chairs on to the set from the terrace for the final scene, the obligatory denouement in the library in which Alexander Cameron would go over the evidence and the culprit would be revealed; a typical country house murder story of that period but effective just the same.

'And that's the lot,' Noel announced. 'The stage's going to be bloody crowded for that last scene with everyone on set except Oliver but it can't be helped. I could've done with a proper dress rehearsal as well but there won't be time for people to change. We're going to be pushed as it is, fitting everything in. There's a reception on the lawn tomorrow evening before the play so they'll have to get used to wearing the costumes at that. Thank God, though, it's short skirts for Annabel and Mary Hogarth; I won't have to worry about them tripping up on their hems.' He glanced at his watch again, his face suddenly drawn and haggard. 'Oh, Lord, it's gone seven! We're going to be late for supper. Is there anything else you want to ask, Roz, before we pack it in?'

'I don't think so. I'll cope and so will everyone else. You shouldn't worry so much.'

'If you're going to say "It'll be all right on the night", don't. In the mood I'm in, I might hit you.'

Laughing, Roz stretched up and kissed him on the cheek. 'Do you know, Noel, you're rather a splendid person, taken all in all?'

She meant it genuinely, although the gesture and the remark were also intended to make up to him for everything – his concern about the play as well as Annabel's and Oliver Hampden's treatment of him, even if Noel seemed less aware of these last two instances than she was herself.

He grinned down at her, surprised and touched, his features young again, puckered up with a boy's smile of delighted pleasure.

'You're pretty fab yourself, Roz.'

'Of course I am!' she said lightly. 'And now,' taking his arm, 'you can be ultra-fab and escort me in to supper.'

3

Because the dining-room was out of commission on account of the play, supper was served in the buttery, a large, comfortable room which was used, Noel explained, for casual family entertaining and which had been the original servants' hall.

The meal was an informal affair, eaten at a large wooden table which occupied the centre of the room, Christie and Mary Hogarth doing any necessary waiting on the guests, carrying hot quiches and bowls of salad in from the kitchen where a middle-aged woman, Oliver Hampden's housekeeper, Roz assumed, seemed to be in charge. As for the rest, it was a question of helping oneself to French bread and the opened bottles of wine already set out.

'Grab a chair,' Christie told Roz as she entered. He was wearing a cook's striped apron and, from the grin on his face, was obviously enjoying himself.

Roz did so, glancing quickly round to see who else was there.

Lady Kelling was not present – perhaps the occasion was too informal for her – but Oliver was already seated at the head of the table; Cliff Teague and Mary Hogarth were also in place; Noel, too, had sat down, next to Annabel, of course, to whom he was chatting with an exaggerated, almost desperate animation, smiling too much and passing her bread and salad before she had asked for them as if anxious to put himself in her good books.

As for Annabel herself, she looked bored and faintly exasperated by all this attention.

Someone unknown was sitting next to Annabel, a middle-aged, grey-haired man with a quiet manner whom Christie, seating himself in the chair next to Roz, introduced as Arnold Wyvern, history master at Widford boys' school and a member of the Widford Players, the local amateur dramatic society, who was to play the part of the butler.

A good choice, Roz thought. He had the face for it.

'Where's the new chap?' Christie added, addressing Noel.

'Sorry?' Noel said, breaking off his conversation with Annabel.

'The one who's playing Tranter, the American art dealer. Don't tell me his wife's had a heart attack, too, and he's had to drop out like Maitland.'

Everyone stopped talking and looked in Noel's direction.

'Sorry,' he said again. 'I should've mentioned it. He phoned me this morning to say he'll be along after supper.'

'Good, is he?' Christie asked. 'Knows his lines?'

Noel turned to Arnold Wyvern for support. 'He'll be all right, wouldn't you agree?'

Wyvern said, 'He's the best substitute we could find at such short notice. Noel and I've rehearsed him a couple of times at my house. He's word perfect and knows all the moves. We'll have to see how he makes out at tonight's rehearsal.'

'It's a damned nuisance about Maitland,' Oliver remarked from the head of the table. 'But there's nothing can be done about it. I suppose we should be grateful someone else was willing to take over the role. By the way, Noel, when you spoke to me on the phone about it last week, you forgot to tell me the man's name.'

'Did I? Sorry. My fault. His name's Frank Clayton.'

'Oh, God!' Roz heard Christie say softly beside her.

Oliver laid down his knife and fork. Although his face was expressionless, there was a deliberation about his actions which suggested a cold, controlled fury.

'If I might have a word with you outside, Noel,' he said.

'Of course! Of course!' Noel scrambled up from his chair and followed Oliver out of the room.

As the door closed behind them, there was a small silence

before those left sitting at the table broke into the kind of over-loud and sprightly conversation which follows any social gaffe. Annabel vivaciously discussed the costumes for the play with Mary Hogarth while Arnold Wyvern launched into a monologue directed at Cliff Teague about the Widford Players and their latest production of Rattigan's *The Winslow Boy*.

Teague himself merely listened, his head ducked down so that it was difficult to read his expression but Roz had the impression that he was amused by Noel's discomfiture. It angered her although she could see the reason for it. Noel had got on the wrong side of Teague by being too officious over the sound and lighting effects and the man could hardly be blamed for wanting to get a little of his own back.

Under cover of the chatter, Christie said to her quietly, 'Poor old Noel! Not his fault, of course, but he couldn't have chosen a worse person than Clayton.'

'Why?' Roz asked.

She had the feeling that Christie, too, was finding the situation amusing, but less on Noel's account than on Oliver's, which opened up a whole area of interesting speculation about the relationship between the two brothers.

'Oliver and Clayton had some row a couple of years ago. They've been carefully avoiding each other ever since.'

He broke off as the door opened and the two men reappeared, Noel looking subdued, Oliver smiling and affable as if nothing of any great moment had happened.

Taking his place again at the head of the table, he resumed the role of host, waiting until there was a gap in the general talk before insinuating himself into the conversation from which point he acted as conductor, easing Noel back into the group with considerable charm and tact and even drawing the normally taciturn Cliff Teague to contribute a remark or two.

By the time the meal was finished, the incident appeared to have been forgotten, even by Noel himself; or so it seemed to Roz who watched over him with a sisterly concern.

She also went out of her way to observe Oliver's reaction to Frank Clayton who joined the group in the dining-room where they went to begin the rehearsal. On this occasion, however, her interest was sheer curiosity.

Clayton was a sandy-haired man in his thirties, heavy-jawed and with deeply tanned features as if from working in the open air. He arrived unannounced and stood silently in the doorway, hands in his pockets, unnoticed by anyone except Roz and Mary Hogarth who came forward to meet him and introduce him to the others.

Oliver, who was on the dais at the far end of the room, discussing some detail about the lighting with Noel and Cliff Teague, merely broke off to nod briefly at Clayton.

Clayton nodded back and then Oliver announced generally, 'Now everyone's here, shall we start?'

And that was that. Apart from an obvious coolness between the two men, nothing at all dramatic occurred, not even a change of expression on Oliver's face.

Taking her place on the prompt side behind the curtains, Roz felt a little let down. She had hoped that, for once, Oliver's charm might desert him and he might show some signs of ill-ease.

But that would have been out of character, she realized, as the scene got under way. Oliver Hampden was a good amateur actor with a natural stage presence; a quality she might have expected. Given that talent, it was unlikely he'd be thrown by the arrival – under his own roof, too – of someone he had quarrelled with two years before.

As for Clayton, he disappeared as unobtrusively as he'd arrived and it wasn't until the first act was over and the others had left by the terrace doors for the scene in the garden that she found him hanging about in the hall waiting for his own entrance in the last part of the play, as she made her way to Oliver's private office.

Nor was there any sign of Oliver who, she assumed, had remained in the dining-room for the beginning of the third act.

After that, she forgot both of them. Her attention was fixed on what she could see happening in the garden through the open window, waiting for her cue to fire the prop gun.

Watching the scene being enacted by the pool, she could

understand both Noel's and Oliver's eagerness to use the outdoor setting, however inconvenient it might be to get the audience out of the house and back again for the last act.

Dusk had fallen and the lighting had been switched on, not just the floodlamps which lit the scene itself but the strings of coloured bulbs which had been looped between the branches of the trees to illuminate the path and which hung among the leaves like clusters of rich, exotic fruit.

It was too far away for Roz to hear the lines which Noel and Annabel were speaking but she was able to follow the action from their gestures.

It was the love scene between Lady Ingsby and Viscount Quest, Lord Ingsby's younger brother; hardly an incestuous relationship but the blood ties were close enough for the book to have caused a sensation when it was first published in 1926.

It was difficult now to understand what all the fuss had been although Roz could see why the novel continued to be popular with the G. B. Russell fans. There was a period charm about the settings and the characters which must have satisfied some deep, nostalgic yearning for the past.

And, in many ways, *The Ingsby Inheritance* was less dated than might have been expected. As Roz had found to her surprise on first reading the book, Russell was a skilful writer with a strong sense of narrative drive and an ability to keep the reader guessing the identity of the murderer until the last chapter.

Although it must have been difficult to adapt into a stage version, Noel had made a workmanlike job of it, cutting out all unnecessary material and concentrating on the plot which had enough action in it to carry the audience along and suspend any critical judgement.

It was a pity, as Roz had often thought, that Noel hadn't chosen to go into the theatre on leaving university rather than the City. He had skills himself both as an actor and as a producer; not West End standard it was true but good enough for most provincial companies to have welcomed his talents.

Watching him through the window as he acted out the love scene with Annabel, she was struck again by the way in

which, once on stage, he managed to shed all those exasperat-
ing qualities of adolescent self-consciousness and the overeager desire to please and impress others and to become
absorbed into the part of the ardent but guilty lover.

Or was it all acting?

Seeing him take Annabel's hand and look into her eyes
before raising her fingers to his lips, Roz wondered if he might
not be in love with her after all; properly in love, that is, and
not just temporarily infatuated as he had been with all the
others.

As for Annabel, she was not bad as an actress but not the
natural that Noel had made her out to be; and that was another
of his weaknesses. When he fancied himself in love, all his
geese tended to be swans.

The scene was coming to an end. Annabel was breaking free
from Noel's embrace, gesturing to indicate the arrival of the
butler; Noel made his exit towards the courtyard, leaving
Annabel alone by the pool to meet Wyvern. The cue came
soon after Wyvern's line: 'A Mr Cornelius Tranter has arrived,
my lady. I've shown him into the drawing-room.'

As Annabel started to walk back towards the house, there
followed a little bit of stage business to give her time to reach
the terrace. It involved Wyvern rearranging the garden chairs
and removing the champagne glasses from the table to place
on a tray.

Leaning out of the window to make sure that Annabel had
reached the terrace steps, Roz fired the prop gun.

It made a satisfactory report, loud enough to be heard in the
garden. Then, without waiting for Wyvern's line, 'Oh, my
God, what was that!' or for the lights to dim and the music to
fade in, she made her way back to the dining-room, the gun in
her hand, in readiness to arrange the set for the final act.

Oliver Hampden was already there, standing at the terrace
doors, the curtains looped back so that he could watch the
scene in the garden.

'You won't be able to do that tomorrow night,' Roz pointed
out, scattering the blackmail letters on the floor round the

41

desk. 'The audience might see you. You're supposed to be dead by now.'

'Yes, I realize that,' he replied shortly as, stepping past her, he took up his position for the opening of the scene, seated in the chair behind the desk, head flung back, his right arm hanging limp.

Without the bloodstained shirt which he would wear for the performance, he looked rather ridiculous, Roz thought with pleasure, as she placed the gun below his right hand and checked the set quickly.

The desk lamp was switched on, the front-of-house tabs closed. All that had to be done was to loop the curtains back from the doors with their cords where Oliver Hampden had disarranged them, and make sure that the doors themselves were left ajar to allow the others to enter without fumbling with the handle. Doors on stage could be hell.

Teague slipped in from the terrace and took his place behind the screen, ready to fade in the opening music, the bitter-sweet melody of Coward's 'The Party's Over Now'.

Assume the audience is settled, Roz told herself, and then cue in Annabel who should be waiting on the terrace to make her entrance. She tapped on one of the glass panes in warning before taking her own place on the prompt side where she began to pull on the cords which controlled the curtains.

To give Cliff Teague his due, he had rigged them up to work beautifully, drawing silently and easily apart by slow degrees to reveal with the maximum dramatic impact the set with Lord Ingsby's body slumped in the chair, facing the audience, the gun on the floor at his side.

Annabel made her entrance through the terrace doors, but too soon and too theatrically.

Noel, who now in his role as producer was seated in the auditorium on one of the gilt chairs, was quick to pick it up.

'Not so fast, darling. Let the audience have time to take in the scene. Remember what I told you? Give it a count of five before you make your entrance. And not so much of the hands-clasped-to-bosom stuff. You're not playing Little Nell. OK, everybody. Let's run through the opening again.'

It worked better on the second attempt although Annabel was still over the top, in Roz's opinion. On this occasion, Noel let it pass, apart from making a note on the pad he carried with him. Knowing his methods, he'd make Annabel go over her entrance again after the full rehearsal was over.

Roz, who had nothing to do in this scene except prompting, felt relaxed enough now that the play was under way with no major hitches to follow the scene more closely and to observe the various actors taking part.

Clayton, as the American art dealer, made his entrance from the back of the room, accompanied by Wyvern as the butler; a clever piece of production technique on Noel's part for it saved overusing the terrace doors, the only other means of entering or leaving the set.

And Clayton wasn't bad either although she wondered what the audience would make of his accent which was overlaid by a local Essex intonation.

Well, it couldn't be helped. At least he knew his lines and no one would be expecting a Royal Shakespeare Company production.

Noel, too, had joined the actors on stage in his role as Viscount Quest just before Wyvern returned to announce that on Lady Ingsby's instructions he had telephoned the nearby residence of Sir Edgar Wellborough, where it was understood Alexander Cameron was staying as a house guest, and the famous private detective was on his way to Highwood House by motor car.

The scene ended shortly after Christie's entrance.

It was much too soon to be realistic. If this was a real murder, Roz thought, the police would take much longer than a few minutes to get there. But in a play such as *The Ingsby Inheritance*, reality hardly mattered and the arrival of Alexander Cameron almost on the heels of the butler's announcement seemed believable.

Christie also made his entrance from the back of the room and was inclined to treat his part as something of a romp, overacting with gusto and assuming an exaggerated upper-class drawl.

43

Roz saw Noel frown and, as soon as the scene was over, was quick to take him up on the point.

Christie laughed but had the grace to apologize and, when the final scene began, the denouement in the library in which he, as Cameron, went over the evidence and revealed the identity of the murderer, Roz noticed that he had accepted Noel's criticism and toned down his performance although he still tended to take some of his longer speeches too quickly.

As she drew the tabs on the final scene, another slow close during which the actors held their positions to form a stylized tableau, immobilized at the moment of revelation, a spatter of applause, too loud for one person, broke out from the auditorium. Roz was aware that Oliver, as soon as his part in the play was over, had seated himself on one of the chairs to watch the rest of the performance, but she had not realized that he had been joined by anyone else.

Opening back the curtains to allow Noel to address the company generally, she noticed that Lady Kelling was now seated at Oliver's side. As Oliver came forward to join the others on stage and Roz moved off the set to give them more room, she was surprised to see Lady Kelling beckon to her, indicating that Roz was to sit beside her. She had not imagined that Lady Kelling would want her company.

But it appeared that she did; and to discuss one particular subject – Annabel Thorpe.

After a few preliminary remarks about the play in general – how good she thought the production was and what a lot of work must have gone into it – she suddenly said, 'Tell me about Miss Thorpe. How well do you know her?'

'Hardly at all,' Roz replied. 'She's Noel's friend, not mine.'

She wondered why Lady Kelling should want to quiz her over Annabel Thorpe as she clearly was doing. The question, though casually asked, was deliberately chosen. So, too, was her next query.

'Is it a long-standing relationship?'

'Noel and Annabel's? No; they've only known each other for a couple of months.'

'I see.' The remark was spoken in a dry, clipped tone. There

44

was a short silence and then Lady Kelling added, changing the subject, although with that disapproving note still in her voice, 'What a pity Mr Maitland had to drop out of the play.'

And that was that.

Lady Kelling said no more and, from the closed look about her profile, Roz realized the short exchange was over. She, too, had been dismissed along with Annabel Thorpe and Frank Clayton.

Roz, who had been listening with half an ear to Noel's comments to the cast, was now able to give him her full attention. He was picking up Christie for speaking too quickly, then Mary Hogarth for not showing a strong enough reaction when Cameron revealed the murderer's identity.

He left Annabel to last.

Roz heard him say, 'I'd like to go over your entrance again at the beginning of act three. You must get that timing right.'

What followed was one of those ridiculous squabbles which, if it hadn't been for the earlier confrontation between Oliver and Noel, might have been put down to general tiredness and quickly forgotten.

'Oh, Noel, must I?' Annabel protested. 'I promise I'll remember to do it properly tomorrow. I'm so exhausted!'

It was at this point that Oliver intervened. 'Yes, can't it be left? I think all of us have done enough for one evening.'

Noel stopped short in the act of pointing towards the terrace doors, frozen into immobility as the actors had been at the end of the final scene.

Under other circumstances, it might have been amusing but Roz found nothing funny in the situation.

She knew exactly what Oliver was up to. He had chosen this moment on purpose to humiliate Noel publicly for the business over Clayton and to demonstrate to everyone present that, while Noel might be the producer, he was still Oliver's subordinate.

Damn him! Roz thought.

She half-rose from her chair, prepared to weigh in on Noel's behalf.

It wouldn't have taken much to tip the balance in his favour.

45

As ASM, she would have been perfectly within her rights to back him up with some comment, spoken lightly.

'I agree with Noel. Another run-through won't take long and I'm sure Annabel won't mind.'

She was too late. Noel had already capitulated.

Lowering his arm, he was saying humbly to Oliver, 'If you say so, we'll pack it in. There'll probably be time to go over the entrance again with Annabel tomorrow.'

Roz subsided on to her chair, her anger directed now at Noel for being so bloody wet.

The group was beginning to break up. Clayton and Wyvern were making for the door. Teague was winding back the tape while Christie had come down from the dais to help his mother to her feet and escort her from the room.

The final part of Oliver's little act was witnessed by those who remained – Mary Hogarth, Teague, Roz herself and Lady Kelling who had paused, her arm in Christie's, and who was watching the last twist to the action with a speculative expression on her face.

Ignoring Noel, Oliver had turned to Annabel. 'All right, darling?' he was saying.

Darling.

If it had been said by Noel, no one would have taken any notice. It was part of his producer's vocabulary and he used it indiscriminately when addressing either Annabel or Mary Hogarth, the only actresses in the play.

Coming from Oliver, it signified a great deal more. It signalled to the others, including Noel, of course, that he and Annabel were lovers.

And it was intended to do so. It was no mere slip of the tongue.

Shoving back her chair, Roz stalked out of the room. It was the only action she dared take. Had she stayed longer, she might have lost her temper.

And what good would that have done? she reasoned with herself as she stamped up the stairs to her room.

It was not her job to fight Noel's battles. For heaven's sake, he was old enough to stick up for himself.

She was willing to bet, though, that as soon as he could get away, he'd be outside her room, wanting to come in and talk.

She was right. She was ready for bed but in her dressing-gown when he tapped at her door, calling out softly, 'Roz, can you spare a minute?' before letting himself in.

He was still fully dressed, apart from the scarf which was missing from the neck of his shirt. Without it he looked denuded and oddly vulnerable, as if part of his personality had been stripped away.

'Of course,' Roz told him although she knew it was going to take a damn sight longer than a minute. 'Sit down.'

He subsided on to her bed, leaning back against the pillows, his arms clasped behind his head, in exactly the position he used to assume when they were students together and he'd seek her out late at night, looking for coffee and commiseration usually also over some love-affair which had gone wrong.

'God, I'm tired!' he said.

He looked exhausted, his face grey and pouched with fatigue.

Without any preliminaries, he said straight out, in a voice that bordered on despair, 'Oh, Roz, what am I going to do?'

'About what?' Roz asked briskly. 'Annabel? Oliver? Or the play?'

'Stuff the play although that's bad enough. I've just done a technical run-through with Cliff to make sure he's got the sound and lighting cues right and do you know what he had the nerve to tell me? That he was choked off with the whole thing. I felt like telling him, join the bloody club. I'd walk out on it right now if it didn't mean letting everyone down. And then there's the business over Clayton. Oliver gave me a proper bollocking over that. How was I to know they'd had some row or other? As for not mentioning his name, that wasn't my fault. Oliver was so impatient over the phone that he didn't give me time to tell him. But never mind all that. It's Annabel I care about. I know there've been plenty of others in the past, but I really love that woman. I'd walk through fire for her. She's different – marvellous . . . Oh, God, I'd've asked her

47

to marry me weeks ago if I thought she'd have me. And now bloody Oliver. . . . !'

He twisted his head away so that he was facing the wall.

He had never wept in Roz's presence but she realized he was close to tears now and she went over to the bed, wondering what she could do or say to comfort him.

Before she reached him, he went on, his face still turned away, 'He's been seeing her in London as well as down here at Cressetts. They've been sleeping together. Cliff told me.'

He would, Roz thought, but held her tongue. There was enough bad feeling without stirring up more between Noel and Teague.

Instead, she asked, 'Does Oliver intend marrying her?'

'God knows. I doubt it. I wouldn't trust him now as far as I could throw him. I wish to hell I could tell him to shove his rotten job.'

'Can't you?'

'What else could I do?'

'Oh, I don't know!' Roz exclaimed, torn between exasperation and concern. 'What about the theatre? You're good at it.'

'Not good enough. In fact, taken all round, I'm not much good at anything, not even the job I've got at the moment. That's why I agreed to do the play.'

'I don't understand,' Roz said.

Noel twisted back to look at her and she saw that he was no longer soft with self-pity but hard and dry with an honesty that she had never seen in him before.

'It's quite simple. I've been passed over for promotion several times now; not quite up to it, I gather; not enough drive and initiative; or so the word trickles down from on high. I thought if I agreed to produce the play, Oliver'd take a more sympathetic line. Arse-licking; that's the expression, isn't it, Roz? Anyway, it seems I'm not much good even at that, judging by tonight's little episode.'

'It's not you,' Roz assured him. 'It's Oliver. He's got this thing about power. He can't help it. He just needs to be top dog all the time.'

'And you saw it straight away,' Noel remarked, swinging

48

his legs off the bed. 'But I didn't. See what I mean, Roz? I'm not as much on the ball as you are over things like that.'

It was true, unanswerable and devastating.

As Roz stood in silence, Noel went on, 'I'll see the play through but I'm going to steer clear of Annabel and Oliver from now on. It's the only way I can cope; otherwise I might hit him or say something to both of them that I shouldn't. And I don't want to stay on here any longer than I have to. Will you back me up on that? You could make up some excuse why we ought to leave tomorrow night as soon as the performance is over and not stay on for the party. It'd sound better coming from you.'

'Yes, all right,' Roz agreed, as she walked with him to the door although, as she kissed him on the cheek, she could not help thinking that, for all his newly acquired self-awareness, Noel still hadn't the courage to confront Oliver directly and was relying on her to extricate him from the situation.

4

Noel seemed normal at breakfast the following morning; a little subdued and distracted but that could be put down by the others to preoccupation with the play rather than any lingering resentment towards Oliver.

In fact, only Christie and Cliff Teague were there when Roz and Noel came down for the meal which, like supper the previous evening, was an informal affair, with people arriving at their leisure to help themselves to cereal and toast or eggs and bacon kept warm in a heated serving wagon.

Mary Hogarth arrived late, having driven over from Widford and Annabel only put in an appearance when everyone else had almost finished.

Oliver, thank God, didn't appear at all, an absence which was explained when Christie addressed them.

'Sorry Oliver isn't here. He's tied up on the phone – some business matter or other. Anyway, he's asked me to go over today's itinerary with you. The memorial service will be held at half past ten. We're to meet at the church gates at twenty past. The members of the Cameron Club will be driven over from Widford by coach. Then it's back here for eleven; coffee in the Stone Gallery where Oliver will give a short talk about G.B. After that the guests are free to look round the gardens and G.B.'s study. At half past twelve, they'll be taken off to Measton for lunch at the Red Lion and a visit to Worleigh Abbey, the setting for *Dangerous Connections*, then back to the hotel for tea. Our own lunch and tea will be served in here. Otherwise you're free for the rest of the morning and the afternoon.

'The audience'll be coached back here for seven and Oliver suggests we're all in costume by then. There'll be a champagne reception in the garden where there'll also be photocalls. Several magazines are going to do features on the Festival. The play will start at eight. Wyvern, as butler, will usher the audience into the dining-room. Once the play's over, it's back to the Stone Gallery for the buffet supper which should finish at about midnight. Any questions? Noel? Cliff?'

Cliff had no questions but Noel, who could never pass up an opportunity to make his presence known, asked, 'Black tie at the memorial service, Christie?'

'If you have one, yes. But it's not necessary. It's a very short service; hardly a full-scale burial.'

It was said lightly. All the same, as Christie left, Noel remarked to Roz, his expression serious, 'I've brought one with me so I think I'll wear it. Adds a bit of tone. You're going to change, aren't you, Roz? You're not thinking of turning up in those jeans?'

He seemed to have recovered. Roz laughed as she got up from the table.

'I was just about to put on full mourning,' she assured him.

They met in the courtyard from where they walked to the church, Noel in his best dark grey suit and the black tie, Mary Hogarth looking dramatic, like a bereaved Andalusian gypsy, in a full black skirt and a white blouse. Roz had compromised by putting on her blue linen dress, the one she wore for staff meetings at Rushdene College.

There was no sign of either Cliff Teague or Annabel and, at the insistence of Noel who was fussed about being late, they set off without them for the short walk down the drive to St Michael's Church.

Oliver's silver BMW passed them on the way, driven at a snail's pace, Oliver at the wheel with Christie beside him, Annabel seated in the back with Lady Kelling, which explained her absence from the group.

If Noel noticed her presence in the car, he made no comment on it. He was explaining to Roz in that proprietorial tone of voice, as if any detail regarding the Hampden family was

51

worth repeating, 'The church used to be in the living of the Cressett Manor, that's why it's built practically on the doorstep. Actually, it's rather fine; mainly Norman with some later additions. It's a pity the service couldn't be held in the church itself. The Cressett family chapel would've made a super setting.'

As he was speaking, Teague came hurrying along the drive to join them, wearing a navy blue pin-stripe suit which Roz suspected was one of Oliver Hampden's cast-offs. It was too wide in the shoulders to fit him properly and Teague looked uncomfortable and oddly diminished inside it.

'Last-minute hitch with some of the sound equipment,' he explained to no one in particular. 'But it's all right now. I've fixed it.'

Noel looked as if he might take Teague up on this but there was no opportunity.

They had arrived at the church where the coach was drawn up on a patch of grass on to which it was debouching its occupants, mostly elderly or middle-aged and the majority of them Americans.

They seemed a prosperous lot, Roz thought, looking them over critically as a prospective audience; well-dressed; obviously well-heeled and full of that indomitable transatlantic energy which the English tend to find so intimidating.

According to Noel, who made a point of knowing such details, the visit to the G. B. Russell Festival was only part of a ten-day literary tour which to Roz sounded surprisingly wide-ranging in its choice of authors. They had already done Dickens's London and Hardy's Wessex. The following day they were due to set off for Stratford-upon-Avon before going on to the Brontë and Catherine Cookson country.

They were also clearly prepared to enjoy themselves and to make the most of what was on offer.

She heard enthusiastic voices raised, remarking on the church – 'Isn't it darling?' – as well as the cute village and the weather.

'I thought it always rained in England,' one American matron was commenting loudly. 'But it's just perfect!'

52

Oliver had already arrived and was moving among them, introducing himself and the rest of his party, at the same time assembling them into some kind of procession with the assistance of their tour guide. Even Roz had to admire the skill with which he managed to smile, shake hands, exchange a few remarks while ushering them into line.

And his timing couldn't have been better.

It was exactly half past ten when the procession was finally formed, the Hampden family at its head, Lady Kelling between her two sons, Oliver on her right carrying a laurel wreath of the same shape and size as the one used every year at the last night of the proms to adorn the bust of Sir Henry Wood.

Annabel Thorpe stood a little to the rear; not quite family but almost.

She was wearing a black and white silk dress and a black hat with a white ribbon, and looked, as Roz had reluctantly to admit, very distinguished, very much the Lady of the Manor.

As the stable clock at Cressetts struck the half-hour, clearly audible through the still air, the vicar arrived and the procession moved off, following the path round to the rear of the church where a newer area of grave-yard extended beyond the original burial ground in which the old headstones leaned at angles among yew trees and wild rose bushes.

Russell's grave was at the side of the path, the grass round it trimmed but still lying in sweet-scented swathes. Beyond lay other memorials, some well maintained like his, others already overgrown with cow parsley and purple vetch.

His was a solid white marble slab, plain apart from a narrow kerb running round it and a headstone in the inevitable form of an open book, one page devoted to G. B. Russell's name and dates, the other to his wife's, who had predeceased him.

A small group of people from the village had already gathered, together with photographers and reporters from the local newspapers, but they were keeping their distance, leaving the members of the official party to collect round Russell's memorial. They did so a little self-consciously, not sure what was expected of them and trying discreetly to jockey for the best view without trampling on the adjoining graves.

The service was short, a reading of the parable of the talents from St Matthew's gospel and a prayer of thanksgiving for Russell's life and work. Then Oliver Hampden stepped forward to prop the laurel wreath against the white marble book; he remained there for a moment, head bowed, in silence.

And then it was all over. The vicar shook hands, the Hampden family stood for photographs in front of the Russell grave and the group began to disperse.

Noel, walking back to the churchyard gate with Roz, was inclined to be critical.

'The whole thing lacked drama. I told Oliver he should have had the church bells; just a single one tolling when the wreath was laid followed by a peal when everyone left – sort of joyful and uplifting.'

'Like a wedding?' Roz suggested and then wished she hadn't said it. She thought of Oliver and Annabel, posing for photographs and looking very much a couple.

Thankfully oblivious, Noel continued, 'Seriously though, Roz, if Oliver intends holding the Russell Festival again next year, the memorial service will want geeing up. I wonder if I ought to mention it to him.'

He appeared to have temporarily forgotten his animosity towards Oliver and Roz wondered if even his decision to leave immediately after the play still stood. She had not yet mentioned to Oliver that she and Noel wouldn't be at the buffet party and decided to wait until later in the day, when she might definitely know Noel's plans, before making her excuses. He could be infuriatingly indecisive at times.

By the time they had walked back to the house, the Cameron Club had already arrived and were installed in the Stone Gallery for coffee and Oliver Hampden's address.

Roz deliberately absented herself although it wasn't entirely possible to escape from Noel who sought her out after lunch for a last run-through on the timing of the play and a check on the props. The scene by the pool had also to be set, a simple matter of carrying two wrought-iron garden chairs and a table into place.

Cliff Teague had already arranged the gilt chairs for the audience on the lawn in a semi-circle of three rows. When Roz and Noel arrived in the garden, he was busy laying strips of artificial grass matting to hide any trailing cables.

Noel loped over to speak to him and Roz took the opportunity to slip away.

There had been very little chance to explore the gardens at Cressetts and she made for an archway cut into a high yew hedge on the far side of the lawn through which she had caught a glimpse of flower borders.

It was a small, enclosed garden, surrounded by the yew hedges and arranged like an Elizabethan knot garden with geometric-shaped beds, edged with box and filled with rose bushes.

On each side stood white-painted benches, set into niches cut into the dense walls of yew, giving the garden the charming formality of an indoor setting transferred to the open air.

As Roz entered, she saw that Christie was lying stretched out at full length on one of these benches, his head cushioned on his clasped hands on one arm rest, his feet up on the other.

He appeared to be asleep and she was about to walk away when he sat up, swinging his legs down to the ground.

'Don't run off,' he called out. 'Come and join me,' adding with a grin as she sat down beside him, 'who are you escaping from? Noel?'

'I'm afraid so,' she admitted, returning his smile.

She was strongly aware of his physical presence, of his arm which was lying behind her along the back of the bench and of the nearness of his face. He exuded a physical self-assurance, less urbane than his brother's but to Roz more attractive for that very reason. There was an irresistible energy about him and a powerful aura of sensuality which told her he would make a good lover.

And if he asked her to go to bed with him, Roz thought, she would probably be enough of a fool to say yes.

'Roz?' he said in a musing tone. 'Short for Rosalind?'

'Yes; my mother once took the part in a college production of *As You Like It* which was where she met my father. He was playing Orlando.'

'And were you born under a star that danced? Or was that Beatrice in *Much Ado*? No, don't answer that. I'd hate to have the image ruined. Tell me about yourself. What does Roz the star do for a living?'

He was flirting with her, Roz realized, but it was done lightly and with an amused air as if he were skilled at the game but refused to take it seriously.

'Not dancing, I'm afraid,' she said, responding to his mood. 'Something much more down to earth. I teach English to foreign students.'

'Ever felt like a change?'

'To do what?'

'Publishing. I could easily find you a place in my firm. I like people who twinkle.'

'I'm not sure. I'll think about it,' Roz said.

She had the feeling that, if she wasn't careful, Christie with his Hampden charm would sweep her into all kinds of commitments, including, no doubt, his bed.

It was an exciting prospect but one she wasn't yet prepared to accept. Some small voice of common sense warned her to wait and see.

Not at all abashed, Christie smiled at her as if certain of the final victory before exclaiming with a sudden change of subject, 'God, I love this place! Look at it!'

He flung out an arm, encompassing not only the garden in which they were sitting but the view of Cressetts above the yew hedge with its irregular lines of tiled roofs and steep gables, the clusters of tall chimneys in patterned Elizabethan brickwork standing proud above them like groups of elaborate chess pieces.

'I used to live here as a child,' he continued, giving her a small, sideways grin as if apologizing for his earlier outburst. 'That was after my father died and before my mother remarried. It was like paradise to me. Old G.B. was very good with children. There were picnics and ponies to ride. And Christmas was like something out of Dickens, only better because it was real. There was always a huge tree in the Stone Gallery which reached up to the ceiling, covered in lights and silver glitter, and we always had charades in the evening. G.B. kept a box of dressing-up clothes in one of the attics, full of tinsel crowns and old velvet curtains we used as cloaks. Can you imagine it? I wish my two sons could have grown up here. They've missed out on so much.'

'It's a pity they couldn't,' Roz agreed.

He hardly seemed to hear her. His eyes still on the view, he continued, 'I know what I'd do if the place were mine. I'd sell up in London and move the publishing firm down here. There's plenty of outbuildings which could be turned into offices. A couple of fax machines, some photocopiers and a few computers and word processors, that's all it'd need. "Cressett Publications." How does that sound to you?'

'It sounds fine,' Roz said at the same time thinking: he's serious about this. He's got it all worked out, down to the name. Out loud, she asked, 'But wouldn't the place be expensive to keep up?'

'Not necessarily. There's a trust fund which G.B. set up to help with running costs. It can't be touched except for maintenance and repairs. A shrewd old boy was my grandfather. He bought the place for a song during the Depression in the 1930s and spent a lot of his money putting it back to rights.'

'And what about your wife? Wouldn't she object if you moved down here?' Roz said. It was nothing more than a game, of course, but she was curious to see how far he'd take it.

'Oh, Caro wouldn't mind. If she did, she could get a small flat in London and come down for weekends. We don't live in each other's pockets. The boys are at boarding-school so it wouldn't interrupt their education.' He picked up one of her hands, turned it over so that it lay palm upwards in his and added, laughing, 'You could come down, too, Roz, if you wanted to and we could sit out here and drink champagne and count the stars.'

It was a quotation from the play, the love scene in the garden, and was spoken with an amused air. In replying, Roz kept her own voice light and casual.

'We ought to do that in the proper setting, by the pool. And where is Oliver supposed to be while all this is going on?'

He looked down at her hand, folding her fingers into her palm. 'Oliver? Oh, he wouldn't be here. Where shall we send him? Never-Never Land? Or to the banks of the great, grey-green, greasy Limpopo river, like the Elephant's Child? No, Florida, I think. It's his kind of setting and there he'd live happily ever after, like Croesus, surrounded by gorgeous women and pots and pots of even more gorgeous money.'

There was an ironic lift to his voice as well as the corners of his mouth as he spoke and Roz felt suddenly uneasy. The game, despite its references to childhood myths and stories, had taken on a more serious tone.

She said, hoping to bring the conversation back to reality, 'He might want to marry one of the gorgeous women and bring his own children up at Cressetts.'

'Oh, Roz, you are a spoilsport!' he protested with mock sorrow. 'You've ruined the game. Or are you playing one of your own? I rather think you might be. All right. I'll join in. Who did you have in mind?'

'Annabel?' Roz suggested. For Noel's sake, it would be interesting to hear Christie's opinion.

'No; not Annabel.' He sounded quite positive.

'Why not?'

'Because Oliver's very careful about image. After all, that's his job. And I doubt the lovely Annabel carries enough clout either financially or socially.'

'She's the daughter of Bernard Thorpe, the financier.'

Roz regretted the remark as soon as she made it and saw Christie's reaction. She had no business to be sitting there, discussing Oliver and Annabel. She had after all been drawn into a conspiracy with Christie which he had signalled the day before when she had first arrived at Cressetts, although she comforted herself with the thought that Annabel's family background was hardly a secret. Noel himself had been eager to tell her about it.

Relinquishing her hand, Christie said softly, 'Is she now? I didn't know that. In her case then, Oliver might make an exception.' He broke off as Noel appeared in the opening in the yew hedge and came towards them.

'Oh, there you are, Roz!' he called out in an aggrieved voice. 'I've been looking for you everywhere. Mary says tea's ready and would everyone please come.'

He stood over them, clearly surprised to see them together and, as Roz accompanied him from the garden, leaving Christie to follow later, Noel asked curiously, 'What were you two talking about?'

'Oh, this and that,' Roz said, shrugging. 'Cressetts mainly. He loves the place.'

'Yes, I can understand that.' Noel was clearly not interested for he went on, 'And talking of Christie, that reminds me. In that final scene, would you signal to him from the prompt corner if he takes his lines too quickly? Get him to slow down. I'll have a word with him about it over tea.'

It was a pity, Roz thought as they walked together towards the house, that she couldn't confide in Noel. She would have liked someone to whom she could have expressed her uneasiness over her conversation with Christie; not just her own attraction to him but other matters as well. There was Christie's obvious desire to own Cressetts which had passed beyond the stage of mere daydreams. She sensed an underlying rivalry between the two brothers, perhaps even a dislike on Christie's part for Oliver. He certainly appeared to have no illusions regarding his elder brother.

And then there were his remarks about Annabel.

What exactly had Christie meant when he spoke of Oliver making a possible exception in her case? Exception to what? Was he implying that Oliver might marry her?

She took a sideways glance at Noel who was still going on about the play.

No; he was the last person she could discuss it with. He was too closely connected himself with that particular relationship.

Thank God, she thought, that in a few hours the play would be over and they could pack their bags and go home, leaving behind all these family tensions and complications.

5

It had been arranged that immediately after tea – another informal meal served on a help-yourself basis in the buttery – everyone would be free to rest until it was time to change into costume and return downstairs by a quarter to seven to meet the members of the Cameron Club, who would be brought by coach from their hotel in Widford. The Hampden family and the other members of the cast were expected to join them for champagne and cocktail snacks on the lawn.

At eight o'clock, the play was due to begin.

Roz spent the intervening time in her room with her feet up on the bed, an improvised DO NOT DISTURB notice which she had printed in large lipstick letters on a sheet of paper hanging from the outside knob of the door.

Even Noel wouldn't dare to ignore it, however much he might long to burst in on her to discuss some aspect of his latest *Angst* – Oliver's treachery, Annabel's defection, the uncertainty of his position at Hampden and Brownlow's or some new concern regarding the play.

Once she was back in London, she promised herself, she'd give him all the time and attention he needed. For the moment, she wanted nothing more than to rest and let the whole lot of them, the Hampden family as well as Noel, go hang.

All the same, it wasn't easy to dismiss Noel entirely from her mind. She fretted about him even while she tried to persuade herself that it would be all right in the end. It usually was. She had seen him through other crises almost as bad as this one from which he'd bounced back with no visible scars.

At six o'clock she got up, barely rested. Having showered, she changed into the black sequinned dress which, as she wouldn't need it for the play and would probably not be staying for the party, was hardly worth putting on for the reception on the lawn. But it would be a pity not to use it. As for stage make-up, that wasn't necessary either.

Over tea, she had offered to help Annabel Thorpe and Mary Hogarth with their costumes and make-up, and was grateful now that Annabel had turned her down, making it quite clear that, as fashion writer for *Rave*, she was quite capable, thank you, of managing both.

It had been said with a smile which hadn't quite disguised the patronizing manner behind the refusal.

Roz was past caring. If Annabel chose to assume this superior attitude, as if she were already mistress of Cressetts, then good luck to her. It had merely confirmed her own belief that Noel was well shot of the woman.

By the time Roz arrived downstairs in the hall, where it had been arranged that they should all meet, the others, with the exception of Annabel and Lady Kelling, were already waiting and in costume, Oliver Hampden, Noel and Christie in evening dress, Wyvern in a butler's winged collar, black trousers and tails, Clayton who, as the American art dealer, was presumably assumed to be less aristocratic in the matter of taste, in a checked sports jacket and plus fours.

The men looked distinguished, especially Christie who was carrying the long black cloak and the silk hat in which he was due to make his entrance as Alexander Cameron.

He caught Roz's glance as she joined the group and winked extravagantly as much as to say, 'Isn't all of this absurd?' once more drawing her into his magic circle.

It was all part of the Hampden charm, of course, which she distrusted so much in Oliver. Even so, Roz found herself smiling in acknowledgement of his amusement before attaching herself to Mary Hogarth.

Something had happened to make her look so old and

haggard, and it wasn't just the costume and make-up although these didn't help.

In her role as Lord Ingsby's middle-aged secretary, she was wearing an unflatteringly straight-skirted black dress and her hair, which had been drawn back into a tight bun, was liberally brushed with grey. Someone, presumably Annabel, had been too heavy-handed with the Number 16 in shading in the age lines and hollows in her face.

Roz was about to make some small, pleasant remark in order to draw Mary Hogarth out and show her that someone cared when a stir of interest and acclaim ran through the group, heads turned and, following the general movement, Roz looked up to see Annabel descending the staircase.

To give the woman her due, Roz thought wryly, there was nothing anyone could teach her about making an entrance.

She came down the stairs slowly, one hand on the banister rail, the other trailing languidly at her side and carrying a fan of turquoise feathers, a shade darker than her dress but exactly matching the aigrette plume in the velvet band which encircled her forehead and which had taken so much effort to find in Widford.

Even Roz had to admit that it had been worth it.

The dress of slipper satin had an iridescent sheen about it which one false colour would have killed and which only a woman with Annabel's figure and pale-gold colouring could have worn successfully. She glittered in it and she knew it.

And then, as she reached the bottom of the stairs and Oliver hurried forward to meet her, Lady Kelling made her own entrance.

It was as beautifully timed as Annabel's; better in fact, for it upstaged hers and was, Roz suspected, designed for that very purpose, uncharitable though it might be to assume that someone of Lady Kelling's age and presence should have deliberately planned such a stratagem.

Her voice preceded her, imperious and decisive. 'Oliver, your arm, if you please!'

She came tapping her way into the hall, erect and severe in black silk, a diamond necklace glittering like a chain of office about her neck, the white hair plaited and piled high into its coronet.

The cast quickly re-formed itself, Oliver hurrying forward to his mother's side while Christie offered Annabel his arm. But it was Lady Kelling who, escorted by her elder son, led the way out of the house and into the garden in time to greet the members of the Cameron Club who arrived shortly afterwards.

Roz was amused to see how rapidly the Cameronians divided into three courts, one paying homage to Lady Kelling whose age and title evidently counted, certainly among the older Americans in the party; another, largely female, formed itself round Oliver Hampden while Annabel Thorpe queened it in the middle of her own, exclusively masculine circle.

Between these groups the waitresses passed serving champagne.

It was when Oliver called for the photographs to be taken that Roz excused herself and moved away towards the edge of the crowd. No one seemed to notice her departure, not even Noel who was talking animatedly to a trio of American matrons, dressed as 1920s flappers in short skirts, one of them smoking a cigarette in an extravagantly long holder. Noel was at his boyish best, laughing a great deal and crinkling up his eyes.

He was putting on a damned good show but Roz was reminded of one of her grandmother's phrases: there'll be tears before bedtime.

There was a nervous excitability about his behaviour which made her uneasy. It could, of course, be merely anxiety about the play although it struck her as significant that he had chosen to stand with his back to Annabel and Oliver.

She wondered again if she ought to tell Oliver that she and Noel would have to leave before the party but decided to postpone making her excuses until she had had the opportunity to discuss it once more with Noel. In his present mood, there was no knowing what his decision might be.

After the late evening sunlight and chatter of voices in the garden, the dining-room struck her as cool, silent and at first empty.

She entered from the hall, passing between the rows of vacant chairs towards the stage which was set for the first act but was not yet lit. It was only when she climbed the steps on to the dais that she was aware that Cliff Teague had arrived before her and was bending down over the console behind the screen on the OP side.

He glowered round at her over his shoulder as she approached.

'Sorry,' Roz said casually, not really meaning it. After all, she had as much right to be there as he had. 'I want to check the props.'

Teague said nothing, merely turning back to his equipment. Presumably he, too, was making a last-minute check on the sound effects for a phone bell rang several times, on the first occasion causing her to start a little at the unexpectedly shrill peal.

After that she ignored both him and it, concentrating instead on her own task as she ran through her prop list.

Inkwell to the left of the desk. Blackmail letters in the top drawer ready for scattering on the floor at the beginning of the third act. Bloodstained shirt which Oliver Hampden would have to change into also at hand in the bottom drawer. Desk lamp switched on.

Moving across the set to the glazed doors, she checked that they were ajar, lingering there for a few moments to take in the view of the garden.

The reception was still going on. Little groups of people stood about on the lawn, the women in their brightly coloured dresses, the men in black evening clothes. Behind them, the sun was beginning to dip below the trees, flooding the sky with a deep mellow light against which the garden, the grass and the figures were transformed into something richer and more significant than just themselves, as if they, too, were part of a much grander production which was being acted out against a huge natural backdrop.

It was like a scene from one of G. B. Russell's own books

come to life, a glance backwards in time to some supposedly golden age of beautiful people drinking champagne in the garden of an English country house, with the added thrill of knowing that numbered among them were the murderer and the victim.

The sound of their laughter and voices coming to her, distanced from across the width of the lawn, added to this impression.

It was ridiculous, of course, Roz thought, briskly turning away from the scene. Like the prop gun and the bloodstained shirt, it was all part of the illusion, a piece of theatrical magic.

Teague, who appeared to have finished checking the wiring to the phone, was standing, hands in pockets, at the far side of the stage waiting, like her, for the audience to arrive and the play to begin.

It seemed uncivil not to say something to him. After all, they were both involved in the production. Besides, with his withdrawn, taciturn manner, she still found him intriguing. She longed to draw him out.

She said, 'I think you've done a marvellous job with the sound and lighting.'

He merely shrugged without looking at her, dismissing her remark.

For an uncomfortable moment, Roz was aware of what he thought of her – a patronizing, middle-class bitch who thought she'd got the right to talk down to him.

But she hadn't intended it that way. She had merely meant to be friendly.

My mistake, she thought. I shan't try that again.

To her relief, Arnold Wyvern entered through the door at the end of the room.

'You two ready?' he called out. 'Because if you are, I'll wheel in the audience. Mr Hampden wants to start as soon as possible, otherwise we're going to run late.'

'I'm fit,' Roz said. Teague, too, indicated he was ready and disappeared behind the screen.

As Wyvern drew the curtains over the two sets of long windows in the auditorium and turned on the overhead lights

65

before leaving the room, Roz took her own place on the prompt side and pulled on the cords which closed the front-of-house tabs. As they rustled together, the set took on that special atmosphere which Roz had always relished. The small, enclosed world of the stage before the audience enters and the play begins had its own claustrophobic magic, bringing with it the feeling that, however familiar the play, anything might happen. Nothing was impossible.

It lasted only a few moments. As Oliver Hampden entered through the terrace doors, Teague faded in the taped music of Noel Coward's 'Lady Be Good' and Wyvern's voice could be heard announcing in his butler's voice, 'This way, ladies and gentlemen, if you please,' as he ushered in the audience. From behind the closed tabs came the anticipatory low buzz of conversation as people found their seats and settled down.

Through a small gap at the side of the curtains, Roz watched their arrival, Lady Kelling escorted to her place in the front row by Wyvern while the others made a dignified scramble for the best seats.

It was almost time. Wyvern was walking back towards the door where he paused to check that the audience was settled, a couple of seconds' grace in which Roz took the opportunity for a last glance over the set with the fatalistic thought that it was too late now to change anything.

Oliver Hampden was in position in front of the bookcase, his back to the audience, the volume of drawings open in his hand. Behind the screen, Teague was perched on his chair, his hands already placed on the console controls, his head turned in her direction as he waited for her signal.

As Wyvern turned off the overhead lights, Roz nodded to Teague who faded out the music, at the same time bringing up the lights on the set. Simultaneously, Roz pulled on the cords and the curtains opened to reveal the library at Highwood House.

It had begun.

And it didn't go at all badly either. In fact, Roz thought it went rather well.

All audiences give off their own atmosphere which the

actors can immediately sense. This one, already mellowed with champagne and the feeling that the play was a special occasion, a one-off event put on entirely for their benefit, was inclined to be sympathetic and appreciative. Roz was aware of the feeling of warm acceptance which came from them, a willingness not to be critical of any amateurish shortcomings on the part of the actors.

And there weren't many, anyway. The only person who showed any signs of nervousness was Mary Hogarth whom Roz had to prompt a couple of times.

Annabel was a little too stagy for Roz's taste but it fitted in more or less with the role she was playing. Besides, she was so beautiful she could get away with anything.

As for the rest, it went without any serious hitches. As the scene ended and Roz closed the tabs over the stage, there was a burst of applause and that spontaneous outbreak of conversation which suggested people were turning to one another to discuss the play.

A few voices rose above the others.

'Weren't they simply wonderful?'

'You'd never guess they weren't real.'

Real actors, Roz supposed the last speaker meant.

It amused her and she thought, I must remember to tell Noel. It'll please him.

Behind her on the stage, Teague was already leaving through the terrace doors to make his way to the pool to take over the lighting and sound effects for the second scene before the audience arrived there. They, too, were departing through the door at the back, escorted by Arnold Wyvern.

Oliver Hampden had risen from the desk, the expression of desperation which he had assumed for the end of the scene replaced by a broad smile of pleasure, so genuine in its delight that Roz felt a touch of camaraderie for the man.

'It went well,' he remarked. 'Didn't you think so?'

'Not bad,' she conceded.

And then he had to spoil it. 'Pity about Mary forgetting her lines.'

'I don't think anyone noticed,' Roz replied shortly and,

deliberately turning her back on him, parted the curtains a half-inch so that she could see into the dining-room.

It was empty, the chairs vacant.

Without turning round, she announced, 'The audience has gone. I'm off, too. The shirt's in the bottom drawer of the desk.'

If he thanked her, she didn't bother to wait to hear it.

Walking quickly, she went down the steps, out of the dining-room and across the hall towards the office. On the way she passed Arnold Wyvern and Clayton standing talking together near the open doors which led into the Stone Gallery.

Behind them she could see the room laid out in readiness for the supper party after the play, the lights turned on and the tables laid with their white cloths and bowls of flowers. Against the far wall, where the long buffet table had been placed, the waitresses from the catering company, also wearing 1920s costume – black dresses, frilly white aprons and starched caps – were putting the final touches to the displays of food under the supervision of the manager.

It was a pity, Roz thought, that she and Noel would miss it. All that smoked salmon and caviare!

But her mind was now made up.

After that last remark of Oliver Hampden's about Mary Hogarth, she was damned if she was going to stay for the party. As soon as the last act was over, she would make her excuses to him and clear off, taking Noel with her – by force if necessary.

Entering the office, she closed the door behind her.

By the time she had crossed to the window, the audience was already in place by the pool and the lights were turned up on the set, illuminating not only the naiad of glittering bronze but another dazzling figure: Annabel, shimmering in peacock blue, and, standing between them, Noel in his black evening clothes, his shirt front gleaming like a white shield.

Leaning her elbows on the sill, the prop gun in her hand, Roz watched them go through their actions with a critical, objective eye.

Oddly, she found she no longer cared about the play. It all seemed as distanced to her as the actors out in the garden. As far as she was concerned, they could all drop dead, except poor old Noel, gallantly kissing Annabel's hand. Like the bitch that she was, she had drawn back from the embrace and was gesturing towards the darkened garden behind the semi-circle of light and chairs where Wyvern would soon come padding out of the shadows to announce the arrival of Cornelius Tranter.

Noel was making his exit towards the house, breaking into a brisk trot as soon as he was out of sight of the audience, head down, shoulders hunched, anxiety stamped on every movement.

Before he disappeared from sight towards the courtyard entrance beyond her line of vision, Roz remembered thinking, The idiot! Why hurry? He's got plenty of time to get back to the house before the third act.

The scene was winding down. Annabel, too, was making her exit, walking a little awkwardly on her high heels, Roz was pleased to notice, across the grass towards the terrace.

By craning her neck out of the window, Roz was able to watch her progress as far as the bottom of the steps which led up to the dining-room and the glass doors.

As she reached them, Roz stretched her arm out of the open window and fired the prop gun.

It had quite a spectacular effect on the audience. Heads turned. Some people started up out of their chairs. Even from that distance, Roz could hear coming faintly towards her across the width of the lawn a ripple of startled consternation followed by a small outburst of relief as the audience realized it was, after all, part of the play, not the sound of a real gun being fired.

Wyvern, bless him, took the situation in his stride, pausing in the act of collecting up the glasses to look towards the dining-room, to focus their attention in that direction while he waited for them to settle down sufficiently for him to speak his last line.

He was in the middle of saying it and the lights had started their slow fade on the scene as Roz left the office, carrying the gun, and crossed the hall again on her way back to the dining-room.

This time the hall was empty and the doors to the Stone Gallery were closed. There was no sign of Noel which surprised her. She had imagined he'd be waiting to waylay her, eager to know what she thought of his big love scene with Annabel.

The only person in sight was Clayton who was standing with his back to her on the porch steps, smoking a cigarette which he dropped to the ground as she passed behind him.

And a good thing, too. It wouldn't do if, when the audience returned, they found one of the cast hanging about, having a quick smoke.

Turning into the short passage which led to the dining-room, she was surprised to see Lady Kelling standing a little further along it, at the door of the room which, on the tour of the house the previous day, Noel had pointed out as being her private sitting-room.

She was in the act of closing the door behind her and had paused for a few moments to grasp her stick more firmly in her hand before walking slowly up the passage in Roz's direction.

'The second scene is over?' she asked.

'Just finished,' Roz replied.

'Then I shall wait in the hall for the audience to come back,' Lady Kelling announced.

Roz made no reply apart from nodding briefly in acknowledgement of the remark. The encounter, short though it was, had delayed her and, although she knew she still had plenty of time to arrange the set for the last act, a feeling of mild urgency overtook her.

Entering the dining-room, she hurried down the aisle between the rows of chairs, mounted the steps in one stride and, parting the curtains, stepped on to the stage.

Her first thought was that Oliver Hampden had fainted.

He was seated at the desk, as if in readiness for the start of the scene, but instead of leaning back in his chair so that as the curtains opened the audience would see the front of his blood-stained shirt, he was lying slumped forward, one arm dangling loose, the fingers brushing the carpet, the other spread wide across the top of the desk.

70

Oh God! Roz thought. What do I do now? Fetch Noel?

No, she decided. In his present state, he'd only panic. Try to bring Oliver round yourself and, failing that, find Wyvern. He'd have to delay the audience anyway and he'd be better than Noel in an emergency.

But what a hell of a time to choose to pass out!

It was with a feeling of resentment that, putting down the prop gun and her prompt copy, she walked round to the back of the desk and placed one hand on Hampden's shoulder, wondering how to lift him into an upright position. He was a big man, too heavy for her to manage on her own.

At the same time, she was struck by his vulnerability. Lying there, sprawled across the desk, he looked curiously *empty* – the word came into her head quite involuntarily, but that was how he appeared.

It was only then, when her hand touched the stretched, black cloth of his evening jacket, that she noticed the cord which had bitten deep into the flesh at the back of his neck.

For a few moments, she stared at it stupidly, her hand still on Hampden's shoulder, unable to grasp its significance but registering with a crazy logic that it looked oddly familiar.

A cord of woven blue silk, tasselled at the ends.

Then it struck her that Oliver Hampden was dead.

She had no conscious memory of how she got off the stage and out of the room, only of running into the hall and of seeing people – Mary Hogarth coming down the stairs, Lady Kelling half-rising from one of the tall-backed, carved chairs where she had been sitting.

And Christie, thank God, who was on the point of coming through the doors to the Stone Gallery.

Seeing her face, he crossed quickly to her side. 'What's happened?'

'It's Oliver,' she said. 'He's dead. I think he's been murdered.'

As he set off at a run for the dining-room, she was aware that Noel was standing just inside the front door, as if he had only that moment entered, and was staring at her, his face as white as a bone.

71

6

Detective Chief Inspector Jack Finch sat on one of the gilt chairs in the dining-room at Cressetts, observing with interest the activities taking place on the small platform at the far end of the room, rather as a member of an audience might watch a stage production.

Indeed, the whole set-up had a bizarre, theatrical quality about it. Beyond the looped-back curtains, the scene was brilliantly lit by a row of lights suspended from a metal gantry as well as pairs of powerful lamps attached to telescopic stands. It was, he supposed, meant to be a study or a library, judging by the props. An old-fashioned upright telephone, pre-war vintage, with a detachable earpiece stood on a desk while on the top of a bookcase a white marble bust – Socrates, was it? or Plato? – gazed out towards the auditorium with a serene, blank-eyed indifference.

With the exception of the murdered man, it was the actors who were out of place. They consisted mainly of the Scene of Crime Officers wearing white disposable coveralls and protective overshoes, who were moving about the stage fingerprinting the furniture and the pair of glazed doors which led out on to a terrace, from where, Finch had been informed, the curtain cord used to strangle the victim, Oliver Hampden, had been taken.

From time to time the set was even more brilliantly illuminated as McCullum, the civilian photographer, took still shots. At the same time, Bretherton was video-recording the scene.

Centre-stage stood Pardoe, the pathologist, who was making his initial examination of the corpse and had taken temporary charge of the production.

It was on his arrival that Finch and his Detective Sergeant Boyce had withdrawn from the scene. The stage was not big enough to accommodate all of them, especially as Pardoe, irascible at the best of times, had been called away from a game of bridge in which he and his partner had been winning.

If the actors didn't fit the set, Finch didn't think much of the dialogue either.

Pardoe was saying snappily, as if any fool could have seen it for himself, 'The man's been strangled, almost certainly from behind and while he was sitting down. There's no sign he put up a struggle; no marks on the hands; no fibres from the cord under his nails that I can see although I'll take scrapings when I do the PM.'

The corpse itself sat upright in the chair behind the desk, looking incongruous and faintly ridiculous. Head and hands bagged, it was dressed in evening clothes and a starched white shirt, the front of which was liberally spattered with blood.

When it had first been heaved into the upright position in order for Pardoe to complete his examination, the blood-stained shirt, together with a gun found lying nearby, had caused a flurry of consternation among the CID officers and the SOCOs.

Even Finch had been taken aback.

Were they dealing with a body on which there had been two attempts at murder, a shooting as well as a strangulation?

If so, what the hell was going on?

But the moment of confusion had passed.

On examination, the gun had proved to be nothing more than a stage prop, its barrel blanked off. As for the blood, forensic tests would no doubt show that this, too, was fake. There was no sign of an entry wound in the chest.

Finch could only assume that the gun and the bloodstained shirt were part of a stage illusion, the significance of which he hadn't yet grasped although he intended doing just that as soon as he had finished dealing with the immediate scene of crime.

So far, he had learnt very little about the murdered man apart from his name and the fact that he had been found dead in the middle of an amateur stage production put on to celebrate the G. B. Russell Festival, whoever Russell was when he was at home.

'Any idea how long he's been dead?' he called out, addressing Pardoe.

The little sandy-haired pathologist came to the front of the stage, peering out past the dazzle of the lights.

'Can't say exactly. He's still warm and there's no sign yet of rigor mortis, not even in the facial muscles. Say a couple of hours but that's only a guess at this stage.'

Which would put the time of death between approximately eight and nine p.m., Finch thought, checking his wrist-watch.

'If some of your men can help get him on to the floor,' Pardoe continued, 'I'll take his rectal temperature. Then, as far as I'm concerned, I'm finished with him until he's on the slab. You can move him whenever you like.'

While this was going on, Finch strolled forward to the bottom of the steps which led up to the stage, and conferred with Wylie, the officer in charge of the SOCOs.

The scene had been photographed, video'd, fingerprinted. Wylie's men had also rolled up the carpet in a paper covering and had taken it away. The clothes and skin of the dead man had been taped and the sticky strips were now attached to Cobex sheets.

Outside on the terrace, beyond the glazed doors, the undertaker's men were waiting with their trolley to wheel the body away.

'Ready?' Finch asked Wylie.

Wylie nodded.

'Then I'll take a last look at him,' the chief inspector announced and, clambering up on to the dais, he stood, hands in pockets, gazing down at the dead man who was now lying in a black body bag, the front still unzipped.

It was his moment of silent communion with the dead.

Oliver Hampden stared back at him, his bloated features, darkly suffused with blood, mercifully softened by the thin plastic bag which covered his head.

There was an angry, glaring intensity about his expression as if he deeply resented the fact that he should have been reduced to this – a mere corpse, grotesquely dead, observed with such close and apparently impassive curiosity by the middle-aged, stocky figure of a detective chief inspector from Chelmsford CID, hunch-shouldered and as undistinguished-looking as a farmer.

Boyce, who had also come forward, remained at the bottom of the steps, knowing better than to interrupt the chief inspector's train of thought although God alone knew what he was thinking. It was impossible to tell. His bland features were expressionless.

A moment later, it was all over.

Finch had moved away, gesturing to the undertaker's men to enter. The zip on the body bag was briskly fastened, the corpse was transferred to the trolley and the small procession set off through the open terrace doors into the night, accompanied by Pardoe who bustled importantly ahead of it, medical bag in hand.

Oliver Hampden had made his last exit, stage right.

'What now?' Boyce was asking, joining Finch on the stage. 'D'you want to get cracking with the interviews?'

Tall, heftily built, the sergeant seemed to tower over the chief inspector, willing him to action.

So far, their own part in the investigation had barely got off the ground, in Boyce's opinion. Apart from a preliminary interview with the dead man's younger brother Christopher Hampden when they first arrived, during which they had established a few basic facts, nothing much else had been accomplished.

This was something of an exaggeration. In fact, Finch had organized the plain-clothes men into drawing up a list of all who had been present in the house at the time when the murder had been committed. They were now corralled in a room which Boyce understood was called the Stone Gallery where it seemed some sort of party was to have taken place later that evening.

But there were nearly forty of them altogether, for God's sake, all of whom would have to make a statement and, at the rate they were going, that could take all night.

And yet there was the chief inspector pottering off to peer behind a screen on the far side of the stage.

Boyce followed to look over his shoulder. What he saw didn't particularly interest him.

It was some kind of sound or lighting equipment for use in the play, he assumed – a large, boxlike object with a sloping front which was fitted with several switches. Electric cables led away from it across the floor to a socket-batten on the wall.

'So?' Boyce persisted. 'Who are we going to start with? The brother? Do you want to get a proper statement out of him?'

Finch came to a decision.

Straightening up his shoulders, he made a smart about-turn and marched off towards the steps leading down from the stage, remarking over his shoulder as he went, 'No, not the brother; the girl who found the body. What's her name?'

'Roz Bennet,' Boyce told him, consulting his notebook as he hurried after the chief inspector.

It looked as if things were moving at last.

Roz received the summons to appear before Detective Chief Inspector Finch with some alarm.

Since her discovery of Oliver Hampden's body, she had gone through a whole range of emotions, from stunned disbelief to an appalled awareness of what had happened.

It had been followed by several minutes of blind panic when she realized that Noel was missing.

This had occurred just before the arrival of the police – two uniformed officers in a patrol car who had answered the 999 call which Christie had put through from the office.

More police had arrived later, including, she gathered, the CID who had been sent for from Divisional Headquarters in Chelmsford, eight miles away.

Before this there had been confusion, members of the Cameron Club milling about in the hall, demanding to know what was going on, mixed up with the cast and some of the catering staff who had come out from the Stone Gallery.

In the middle of it all, Lady Kelling had remained seated in the great carved chair, as immobile as a figure from a waxworks, her hand which still grasped her walking-stick so rigid that it appeared part of its engraved knob.

It was Christie who, with Wyvern's assistance, had created some order out of the chaos, ushering everyone into the Stone Gallery before leading his mother away down the corridor to her private sitting-room, Roz assumed.

It was then, as the double doors of the gallery were closed, that Roz realized Noel was missing.

Sitting numbed and bewildered at one of the tables, she tried to recall when she had last seen him and remembered with a jolt of fear that it had been soon after she discovered Oliver Hampden's body. As she ran into the hall, Noel had just been coming in through the front door. She could still see his face, ashen with fear.

But where had he come from and what had he been doing after he'd made his exit at the end of that second scene?

He hadn't been in the hall when she crossed it on her way to the dining-room to set the stage for the third act. She remembered remarking on his absence.

She had not dared think beyond this point, frightened by the implications which her unspoken questions might arouse.

But the facts could not be denied and they rose in her mind in a series of single words or broken phrases.

Oliver and Annabel. Oliver's treatment of Noel during the rehearsal. Noel almost in tears the evening before.

She had a swift and disturbingly vivid image of Noel sitting on her bed, his face turned away from her as he said that he felt tempted to hit Oliver.

She had felt an enormous sense of relief when, about half an

77

hour after everyone had been assembled in the Stone Gallery, the doors had opened and Noel had been ushered in by a uniformed officer.

Looking very white, he crossed over to where she was sitting.

'Where the hell have you been?' she had demanded, anxiety giving her voice an edge of fury which she hadn't intended.

'Sorry,' he mumbled. 'I was out in the courtyard being sick.'

'Sick?' She could believe it. He looked shaky enough, his hands trembling. 'Why?'

'It's Oliver . . . ' he had started to say.

There was no time for him to add anything more. The uniformed man had been joined by several plain-clothes officers who had begun to make a round of the room, taking down names and addresses while the PC took up a position immediately in front of the double doors.

He stood relaxed, feet apart, hands clasped behind his back as if off-duty but his presence was ominous. Quite obviously, no one would be able to leave the room without official permission.

Nor, she realized with a sense of rising dismay, would it be possible to question Noel any further about what he had been doing and where he had been during those five minutes or so after he had come off-stage at the end of the garden scene.

Listen, she wanted to say to him, we've got to think up something between us to tell the police.

She wouldn't have gained his attention anyway. He was leaning forward in his chair, elbows on knees, head between his hands, totally withdrawn into some private world of his own where she knew it would be impossible to reach him without drawing attention to them both.

He was even oblivious of Annabel who, wide-eyed with shock and looking ghastly under her make-up, was sitting on the far side of the gallery where she was being tended by a solicitous circle of Cameronians.

It was shortly after this that the plain-clothes men began escorting those who had taken part in the play out of the room. One of them came and stood over them.

'Miss Bennet?' he asked. 'Would you mind coming with me? Detective Chief Inspector Finch would like to talk to you.'

Realizing there was nothing she could do, Roz followed the man out of the Stone Gallery and across the hall to Oliver Hampden's office where he tapped on the door.

From Finch's point of view, the room was ideal for the purpose of interviewing. It had a couple of telephones and a desk, it was conveniently situated and it had a relaxed, unofficial atmosphere created by the low, beamed ceiling and the comfortable leather armchairs, in a pair of which he installed himself and Boyce, drawing a third round to form an intimate circle. This setting suited his technique of interviewing witnesses and potential suspects far better than the more formal, inquisitorial approach.

'Well, now,' he said, looking up and smiling as Roz was ushered into the room. 'Miss Bennet, isn't it? Come in and sit down. I believe you were ASM for the play.' He had learned that much from Christopher Hampden, the dead man's younger brother. 'Tell me about it.'

Roz seated herself cautiously on the edge of the armchair, not quite ready to relax although she was disarmed a little by the chief inspector's opening remarks, as he had intended her to be.

All the same, she regarded him warily. He was not quite what she had expected. There was an open, guileless look about him which she suspected was deliberately assumed in order to put people at their ease.

'What exactly do you want to know?' she asked. 'The plot? The cast? Who played what character?'

'Anything you care to tell me,' Finch replied cheerfully.

She chose to start with the plot, an interesting decision, Finch thought. It showed a reluctance on her part to get down to the essential facts of her discovery of Oliver Hampden's body, as if she were postponing that part of her statement in order to give herself time to think.

'Well,' she began, 'the play mainly involves Lord Ingsby who's being blackmailed – he doesn't know who by – over a

79

love-affair he had when he was an undergraduate at Oxford. The girl died giving birth to the baby and her parents took the child away for adoption. Because of the blackmail payments and the Wall Street crash, he's short of money and he's secretly arranged to sell some Holbein drawings, part of the Ingsby inheritance. The only person who knows about the sale is his secretary whose brother catalogued the family art collection the previous year. He's an artist and Lord Insgby gave him the job because he was broke.'

This outline of the story sounded absurd even to Roz, although she supposed that most plots, even that of *Macbeth*, would appear equally ridiculous if told in précis form.

For Noel's sake, she deliberately left out any reference to that part of the story which concerned Lady Ingsby's love-affair with Viscount Quest, Ingsby's younger brother, and passed quickly on to the rest of the play.

'Anyway,' she continued, 'Lord Ingsby is found dead at the beginning of the third act. At first it's thought he's committed suicide because of the blackmail but Alexander Cameron, Russell's private detective, is able to show it's really murder.'

She stopped there, as if the word 'murder' had dried up the flow of words.

Finch watched her with an avuncular expression which disguised his real thoughts.

He found her attractive in the black sequinned dress which gave her an air of 1920s frivolity. But she was far from stupid. On the contrary, she was as sharp as a needle and quite capable of covering up the truth if she wanted to.

'And who are the suspects?' he asked to get her going again. Although he had never read any of Russell's books, he knew the type and suspected that there were several characters who could have committed the murder.

'Lady Ingsby, Viscount Quest and Cornelius Tranter, an American art dealer who was going to buy the drawings but who is really Lord Ingsby's illegitimate son and the blackmailer. But, in fact, the murderer turns out to be Miss Carmichael, Lord Ingsby's secretary. Her brother had made copies of some of the drawings and sold the originals. She

80

shoots Lord Ingsby so the truth won't come out. Alexander Cameron is able to prove all this because he's an art expert himself and the paper the copies of the drawings are made on isn't the right sort.'

'Let me get this straight,' Finch said. 'Oliver Hampden, who played Lord Ingsby, was last seen alive at the end of the first act. Am I right?'

'Yes,' Roz said.

It was quite clear that the chief inspector was getting down to the facts of the murder.

'Who by?'

'By me. I left him on the stage in the dining-room.'

'What happened then?'

'The audience left to go out into the garden for the second act which takes place by the pool.'

'And where did you go?'

'I came in here.'

'Why?'

'To fire the prop gun out of the window. I couldn't see the actors properly from the dining-room because there's too many bushes in the way.'

Finch got up from his chair and moved towards the window. He assumed that whatever scene had taken place out there would have been better lit than it was now. Someone had turned off the lights with the exception of some strings of coloured bulbs which were looped between the trees. In their subdued glow, he could just make out a stretch of lawn leading down to a round pool in front of which three rows of gilt chairs had been set out in a semicircle.

The setting, surrounded by trees and shrubbery, formed a natural amphitheatre in which an ornate, wrought-iron garden table and a couple of matching chairs set in front of the pool seemed to be the only props.

'Who took part in the scene?' he asked.

'Noel Fielding and Annabel Thorpe. Noel was playing the part of Lord Ingsby's younger brother as well as producing the play. Arnold Wyvern came on as butler towards the end.'

'Anyone else?'

81

'Cliff Teague. He was in charge of the light and sound effects.'

'And where exactly was he?'

Roz came and joined him at the window, pointing to the clump of shrubbery to the right of the pool. 'He was there, out of sight of the audience.'

'Did anyone from the audience leave before the scene was over?'

'No, no one.'

'You'd've seen if they had?'

'Yes, of course. The lights were on and the whole area was well lit.'

'Who turned the lights off?'

'Cliff Teague. He faded them out as well as the music at the end of the scene as the audience left.'

'What about Mr Fielding and Miss Thorpe? When would they have made their exits?'

Oh, God! Roz thought. What do I say to that?

Desperation seemed to free her imagination and she heard herself saying, 'Oh, they came off shortly before the end of the scene, Annabel stage right towards the terrace, and Noel stage left in the direction of the courtyard. It was soon after that I fired the prop gun out of the window.'

She was lying. Finch, who had seen the look of apprehension on her face before she answered, was convinced of that. But on whose account? Her own or someone else's?

Leading the way back to the circle of chairs, he waited until she had settled herself before asking his next question. 'You were saying, Miss Bennet, that you fired the prop gun at the end of the scene. What did you do next?'

'I went back to the dining-room to set the stage for the last act.'

'Which was when you found Mr Hampden dead?'

'Yes,' Roz said simply. 'At first I thought he'd fainted. . . . '

'We'll come back to Mr Hampden in a moment. I'm more interested in who you saw on the way. You must have gone through the hall. Did you pass anyone?'

82

'Frank Clayton. He was standing on the steps, smoking a cigarette. And I spoke briefly to Lady Kelling.'

'Where was she?'

'Coming out of a room a little further down the passageway. I believe it's her private sitting-room.'

'So she wasn't among the audience for the second scene, the one in the garden?'

'No; I suppose she can't have been.'

Her answer corroborated part of the statement Christopher Hampden had given Finch earlier that evening. Hampden had said that he had remained with his mother in her room for most of the second scene, between the time his brother had last been seen alive and before the discovery of his body.

'Did you see or speak to anyone else apart from Mr Clayton and Lady Kelling?'

Roz hesitated. She was thinking of Noel who hadn't been in the hall as she had expected. To cover up his absence, she said, 'No; but I wasn't taking any particular notice. I was in rather a hurry. I had quite a lot of things to do – scatter the blackmail letters on the floor, put the gun in position, check everything on the desk was in place.'

She was lying again, Finch thought. In his experience, witnesses usually went in for this kind of lengthy explanation when they had something to hide.

He said, his voice a little perplexed as if he hadn't quite grasped the complexities of the situation, 'Let's run over the details once again, Miss Bennet, just to make sure I haven't got them wrong. Miss Thorpe and Mr Fielding were taking part in the scene by the pool and didn't leave until it was almost over when they were joined by Mr Wyvern. Mr Teague was also out there, in charge of the light and sound effects.' He took the list of actors which Christopher Hampden had given him earlier in the evening from his pocket and consulted it. 'That leaves a Miss Hogarth, a Mr Clayton and Mr Christopher Hampden who weren't due to come on until the last act. Am I right?'

'Yes,' said Roz. She was relieved that Finch hadn't questioned her more closely over the timing of Noel's exit. As for

83

the others, she was less concerned about their movements. She couldn't cover up for them all.

'So,' Finch continued, 'they would have been where – somewhere in the house, waiting to make their entrances? Yes? Good! Apart from Mr Clayton, did you happen to see any of them at any time in the hall?'

'Not on my way back to the dining-room but when I left it at the end of the first act, I passed Arnold Wyvern and Frank Clayton on my way to the office. They were standing talking together in the hall.'

'But you didn't see Miss Hogarth?'

'No.'

'Or Mr Christopher Hampden?'

'I didn't see him either until after I'd found Oliver's body. When I ran back into the hall, he was just coming out of the Stone Gallery.'

That also corroborated part of Christopher Hampden's statement. According to him, he'd paid a brief visit to the Stone Gallery in order to check the arrangements for the buffet supper which was to have taken place after the play.

Finch beamed cheerfully at her.

'We're getting there at last!' he exclaimed, apparently pleased with the way the interview was progressing. 'And what would Oliver Hampden have been doing while all this was going on?'

'I'm not sure. I didn't see him after the end of the first act until I – I found him. I assume he stayed in the dining-room. He had to change out of his shirt into the bloodstained one which I'd left in a drawer in the desk.'

'Ready for the beginning of the third act?'

'Yes; that's right.'

'Who'd've found him – in the play, I mean?'

'Annabel Thorpe. Once the audience was back in place, she'd've come in from the terrace where she was waiting to make her entrance.'

'Through the doors on the set?'

Roz nodded.

'But you found him instead? I'm sorry about this, Miss

84

Bennet – it must be very distressing for you – but I need to know exactly what happened from the moment you left the office up to the time you found him.'

She said, 'Well, as I've already described, I crossed the hall towards the dining-room. . . . '

'Seeing Clayton and Lady Kelling on the way?'

'Yes; then I went into the dining-room and on to the stage.'

It was Boyce who asked, 'Were the curtains closed or open?'

'Closed. Oliver Hampden was lying across the desk – unconscious as I thought. I didn't try to lift him; he was too heavy. It was then I saw the cord round his neck and I realized he'd been murdered. I can't remember much after that except running back into the hall and seeing Christie – Christopher Hampden – coming out of the gallery. I told him what had happened and he took over.' Clearly distressed, she added, 'Is that all you want to know?'

Not by a long chalk, Finch thought. There was still a lot more information he wanted from her. But not now. That could wait until after he'd interviewed the others and was a little more sure of the facts.

'Yes,' he said, getting to his feet. 'That's all for the time being, Miss Bennet. Thank you for your help. You've cleared up several points I needed to know.'

Not sure how to take this, Roz glanced at him quickly. But his face had again assumed that bland expression which told her nothing.

'I suppose,' he added with the same guileless air, 'that as you acted as prompt, you'd have had a copy of the play. Could I borrow it? Just to make certain I know what was going on.'

She said quickly, 'Not with me,' thinking, Oh God, he's going to find out when Noel made his exit.

'No? Then there would it be?'

'I'm not sure.'

'Really? But you must have had it with you when you went back to the dining-room to set the stage?'

'Yes, of course. I must have put it down somewhere. I can't remember.'

'On the desk, perhaps? Not to worry. It'll turn up.'

85

He sounded casual as if it didn't really matter to him one way or the other.

But she was quite sure his last question was deliberately timed even though it seemed like an afterthought.

He waited until she had reached the door and was about to leave the room before adding, 'Oh, by the way, Miss Bennet. I forgot to ask. Who in the play takes the part of the murderer?'

There was no ducking that one.

'Mary Hogarth,' she told him.

7

'Sounds like a load of old rubbish to me,' Boyce commented as the door closed behind Roz.

Finch assumed he was referring to the play rather than Miss Bennet's statement although he had his reservations about that as well.

Out loud he said, 'Get hold of Wylie. Tell him there should be a copy of the play somewhere on the stage in the dining-room. It's probably been bagged up as evidence. Say I want a photocopy of it made as soon as possible. He can use the copying machine in here. And while you're at it, find Clifford Teague. I want to have a chat with him out by that pool.'

'Teague?' The sergeant sounded surprised. 'Why him? If he was in charge of the sound and lighting effects, he can't have bumped Hampden off. As far as I can work it out, he's one of the few out of the whole bunch who seems to have an alibi.'

'That's why. I want to check with him who was supposed to be where. And tell him I'd like to see that pool properly lit up, like it was tonight before Hampden was murdered.'

'Right,' said Boyce, making for the door. 'I get your drift.'

In his absence, Finch strolled back again to the window, where he leaned out over the sill as he assumed Roz Bennet must have done in order to fire the gun. He remained there in silent contemplation until the sergeant's return.

Boyce was back within minutes to announce, 'Wylie says he'll get that script photocopied as soon as he can. And Kyle, one of the DCs, is on his way down to the pool right now with Teague. The lights should be coming on any minute.'

87

They went up before he had finished speaking, gradually strengthening in brilliance until the area round the pool was brightly lit. It was now possible to pick out much more detail, including the naked bronze figure of a girl which rose, arms upstretched, from the centre of the water.

The semicircle of chairs was also much more visible and Finch could understand why Roz Bennet had been so certain that no one in the audience had left while that scene was being played. Anyone getting up from his or her seat would immediately be seen from the office window.

'OK?' Boyce asked, meaning was the chief inspector ready to examine the setting and talk to Teague.

But Finch remained where he was for several more moments, head craned out over the sill.

Although the area immediately in front of the pool was lit up, the lights illuminated less of the garden than he had expected from Roz Bennet's statement, another point which made him doubt the accuracy of what she had told him. She had said that she had watched Noel Fielding and Annabel Thorpe leave the set at the end of the scene but, while Annabel Thorpe would have been in her line of vision as she made her exit in the direction of the terrace, the same didn't apply to Fielding.

Once he'd walked up the lawn towards the courtyard, he'd've passed too far to the left for her to see him reach the archway in the wall.

He'd have to confirm his suspicions, of course; get a couple of men to go through the same movements as Fielding and Annabel Thorpe, and see just how far he could follow them from Roz Bennet's vantage point at the office window.

'Right!' He said, turning back to Boyce. He was ready for Teague.

They found Kyle waiting with Teague in the garden, both men standing well outside the lighted area as if too self-conscious to make use of the chairs which had been set out on the grass.

Finch had no such inhibitions. Beckoning them across to the

88

front row, he shifted his chair round so that he was facing Teague, taking the opportunity to glance quickly at the man.

He was thin but wiry, with dark, sharp features that had a closed, taciturn look about them.

'Now, Mr Teague,' he said. 'A couple of questions first about the scene itself. How long did it last, would you say?'

Teague lifted his shoulders. 'I dunno exactly; quarter of an hour; twenty minutes at most.'

'And I gather Miss Thorpe and Mr Fielding were on the set right up to the end?'

'Who gave you that idea?' Teague answered in a jeering manner. He had been sitting with his head bent forward so that all Finch could see of him was a narrow, bony skull, dark hair that was beginning to go thin on top and a pair of shoulders thrust up round his ears. It was a defensive, un-cooperative pose. But as Teague spoke, he lifted his face and Finch saw the dazzle of the lights reflected in his eyes.

'When did they leave the set then?' he asked sharply.

'Several minutes before it finished. Fielding went off first.'

'In that direction?' Finch pointed to the archway in the courtyard wall.

'Yeah.'

'Did you see him go through the arch?'

'No; I wasn't watching.'

'And Miss Thorpe? What about her?'

'She left that way a couple of minutes after Fielding.' Teague jerked his thumb towards the right. 'She was supposed to wait on the terrace.'

'Supposed to?'

'Well, I expect she did then. I wasn't watching her either. She comes in at the beginning of the last act through the terrace doors.'

'So she'd've passed you?'

'That's right.'

There was an ambivalence about Teague's answer which made Finch press him for a more definite response.

'Did she pass you?'

89

'Yeah; of course she did.' Teague seemed amused by the chief inspector's obtuseness.

For his part, Finch felt a sense of rising exasperation towards the man. Short though his answers were, they seemed deliberately designed to confuse rather than clarify the situation. He had met Teague's type before. They were usually men, intelligent and street-wise with some bloody great chip on their shoulders about anyone in authority. Information had to be squeezed out of them, drop by grudging drop.

He crossed his legs comfortably, settling down for a long session.

'Right, Mr Teague. We've got Mr Fielding who's already made his exit to the left and Miss Thorpe going off to the right towards the terrace, which leaves Mr Wyvern as the butler still on the set. What happened next?'

'That woman from London fired the prop gun out of the office window. After that, Wyvern had a line to say which was my cue to bring up the music and begin fading the lights. Then Wyvern started to get the audience back into the house for the last part of the play.'

'And you?'

'Me? After I'd cut the music, I walked over to the terrace.' Again the thumb was jerked into action to indicate the direction he'd taken. 'It was my job to do the light and sound effects for the last act.'

'And by this time Mr Hampden was dead?'

'Yeah. When I got to the terrace doors, Christie Hampden was already there. He told me Oliver had been murdered and I wasn't to come in. So I cleared off round to the front of the house.'

Teague had dropped his head again so that it was impossible to see his face. Even his voice was barely audible.

It was time, Finch decided, for a change of tactics. Getting to his feet, he said, 'I'd like a look at the control board – console, or whatever it's called. It's over here, is it?'

He led the way towards the clump of shrubbery where Roz Bennet had indicated Teague had set up his equipment.

It was a good choice of position. The bushes – rhodo-dendrons, Finch thought although he'd never been much of a gardener – formed a natural hide, a rough, horseshoe-shaped clump, at the back of which a table and a chair had been placed, screened from the audience by the thick leaves.

A tape recorder was standing on the table, wired up to two big loudspeakers on either side of the pool. Next to it was a box about the size of a large attaché case, similar in design to the one he had already seen on the stage in the dining-room. It was equipped with a set of switches which he assumed were for controlling the lights, together with several plugs from which cables trailed down and led away across the grass, protected by lengths of matting.

He stood over it, hands in pockets, his expression interested but a little puzzled.

'You'll have to show me how it works, Mr Teague,' he remarked with a disarmingly frank air. 'When it comes to this sort of equipment, I'm afraid you've lost me. Changing a plug is about my limit.'

He stood back watching as Teague took over at the controls.

'OK. There's two portable lighting stands out there,' Teague said, nodding in the direction of the pool which was visible through a gap in the bushes. 'Each one's equipped with two 500-watt floodlamps, making 2,000 watts altogether. The console can take a total of 2,400 watts so there's no problem of overloading. The lamps are wired up to these socket outlets on the back of the console. When you want to bring the lights up or down, you turn these dimmer switches to the left or right. For a slow fade, you ease them round gently.'

He demonstrated, fading the lights round the pool and then bringing them up again.

'And that switch?' Finch asked, pointing to the console.

'That's the master switch,' Teague told him. 'The whole thing's cabled up to a 13-amp socket in the house. There's a built-in fuse in case anything goes wrong.'

'Clever stuff!' the chief inspector remarked. 'I suppose all of the equipment was hired?'

'Most of it,' Teague replied. After his burst of loquacity, he had clammed up again.

'Where from?'

'Mr Hampden arranged it with some amateur drama group in Widford. Ask Arnold Wyvern if you want to know the details. He fixed it up.'

'I gather you work here as a handyman?'

'That's right.'

'For how long?' The lights had dimmed round the pool so that again it was difficult to see Teague's face and Finch added, 'Turn them up again.' He watched the man's profile as the lights brightened.

'Six, seven years.'

'Good boss to work for, was he?'

'Yeah, he was.' For once, Teague sounded surprisingly positive. 'He didn't interfere; let me get on with things in my own way.'

'Any idea who might have wanted to kill him?'

He put the question in an offhand manner, copying Teague's own style. For several seconds, the man remained silent, looking down at the controls on the console.

Then he said, 'Ask that Fielding bloke. Mr Hampden had been screwing around with his girl friend, the blonde one.'

Interesting his use of language, Finch thought. It expressed a contempt not just for Fielding who, it seemed, had got on the wrong side of Teague in some way but for the woman as well who, from the description, couldn't be Roz Bennet and therefore had to be Annabel Thorpe.

'Anyone else?' Finch asked.

Teague hesitated and then with a more shamefaced reluctance said, 'Mr Hampden had some row with Frank Clayton a couple of years ago. Clayton used to work here as a contract gardener.' He seemed to regret this remark for he added quickly, dissociating himself from the situation, 'I don't know much about it. Is that the lot?'

'Yes; for the time being,' Finch told him.

There was no point in protracting the interview. He'd get nothing more out of Teague that night.

'So can I take this stuff away then?' Teague was asking, indicating the console and the tape recorder. 'If they get damp, it'll muck them up.'

It was sheer perversity on Finch's part to turn him down, his own way of paying Teague back; childish, perhaps, but he didn't feel in the mood to be generous.

'No,' he said. 'Leave them where they are. I haven't finished here yet.'

Teague took the refusal with bad grace, giving the chief inspector a glowering look before slouching off up the lawn in the direction of the house, accompanied by Kyle.

When he had gone, Boyce said, 'What d'you want done round here then? Hampden wasn't even in this scene.'

He followed the chief inspector who had set off towards the lighted area round the pool where he came to a halt.

Finch himself seemed unsure. He was standing hump-shouldered under the floodlights, looking like an actor who had forgotten his lines, contemplating in turn the rows of empty chairs, the lighting stands and finally the figure of the naiad which rose, glistening and naked, from the centre of the glittering water.

'Timing,' he said, with apparent inconsequentiality. 'It's all a question of timing, Tom.'

The thought seemed to wake him from whatever reverie had overtaken him, for he added more decisively, 'I'll get McCullum to take a few shots of this with the lights on before the whole set-up's dismantled. And tomorrow, in daylight, I want a couple of men to go over those exits Fielding and Miss Thorpe made with a tape and a stop-watch; see just how long it'd've taken them to get from here back to the house.'

'Right!' said Boyce. He could see the point of all that.

On their return to the house they were met in the hall by Barney, one of the CID officers, who handed over the photocopy of the play which Wylie had made.

As he gave it to Finch he added, 'We've finished with the witnesses. Everyone who took part in the play's given a preliminary statement and we've got the names and addresses and a brief account from everyone else. Is it all right to let them leave now? Some of them who were in the audience are knocking on a bit and I've had their tour guide round my neck, asking when they can go back to their hotel. We can interview them again tomorrow, if necessary. They're not due to leave for Stratford until the afternoon.'

'Yes, all right,' Finch agreed. There was no point in keeping them hanging about any longer.

It was Christie who made the announcement, coming into the Stone Gallery, accompanied by one of the plain-clothes men. His face and voice strained, he called for their attention.

'I'm sorry you've been kept waiting for so long, ladies and gentlemen. I now have permission for you to go. If the members of the Cameron Club would care to leave first, you'll find the coach waiting outside in the courtyard to take you back to your hotel.'

The news was greeted by relief, especially by the more elderly Cameronians. People began to get up from their chairs and make for the doors into the hall.

'And about bloody time, too,' Roz heard Clayton comment as he pushed past her, his face glistening with perspiration under his make-up.

She ignored the remark, standing on tiptoe to look for Noel who had gone ahead of her through the crowd, his arm round Annabel's shoulder.

But they must have parted in the hall because he was alone when she finally caught up with him on the upper landing.

'Noel!' she called.

He halted and turned to face her. He had taken off his bowtie which hung round his neck, and had loosened the collar of his shirt. In this state of disarray, he looked dishevelled and slightly tipsy.

'Yes, Roz; what do you want?' he asked, his voice slurred. He kept blinking at her rapidly as if trying to keep her in focus. She realized then that he wasn't drunk, only so exhausted that he was having difficulty in standing upright.

'I must talk to you,' she said.

'Oh, for God's sake, not now!' he protested. 'All I want to do is get my head down and sleep for about twenty-four hours.'

'Yes, now!' she retorted and, taking him by the sleeve, dragged him along the corridor to her bedroom where she bundled him inside.

Once in the room, he broke away from her grasp and made for the open window where he stood leaning against the frame. He took several deep breaths of air before, raising his head, he remarked in a sudden little outburst which had the edge of hysteria to it, 'Look! Someone's turned the lights on round the pool!'

'Never mind that,' Roz told him severely. If he hadn't looked so damned ill, she would have shaken him to get some sense into him. 'About tonight. . . . '

'I know what you're going to say,' Noel broke in. 'I may be a fool but I'm not that bloody stupid. Where was I when Oliver Hampden was getting himself murdered? Isn't that what you were going to ask? Well, I wasn't anywhere near the dining-room.'

'Then where were you?'

'You mean after I made my exit?'

'Yes, of course I do!' His evasiveness further angered her. It seemed to her that he was playing for time.

'I walked up the lawn and then stood by that archway into the courtyard.'

Roz wasn't sure whether to believe him or not. If he had been standing there, she hadn't seen him. Her attention had been on Annabel while she waited for the cue to fire the prop gun. In fact, she wasn't sure that the archway was visible from the office window.

'What were you waiting there for?' she demanded.

It was his turn to become angry. 'For God's sake, Roz, isn't it obvious? I'd just finished my big love scene with Annabel. I was watching her. God, she looked beautiful under the lights! Absolutely stunning! And, all right, if you want the truth, I was thinking of her and Oliver and what the hell I should do about it. But I didn't kill him. I was standing by that bloody archway until after Annabel went off and you fired the prop gun. Then I came back to the house. You can't possibly think I did it. I can't stand anything to do with blood or dying. That's

95

why I was sick this evening after Clayton told me Oliver'd been murdered.'

His anger sounded genuine but Roz still wasn't sure how far to believe him.

If only she'd known about Noel's whereabouts earlier in the evening, before she'd made her statement to Finch, she was thinking. She could have cleared him by saying she'd seen him by the courtyard entrance.

'Listen,' she said. 'The police are going to question you tomorrow. Whatever you do, don't say anything about Annabel. Think of some other reason why you waited out in the garden.'

'What reason?' he asked.

'I don't know!' Her imagination failed her. 'Can't you use your own initiative for once? Tell them. . . . '

But he was pushing past her on his way to the door. 'Thanks a whole bunch, Roz! It's good to know who your friends are!'

The door slammed behind him.

Roz was tempted to go after him and then changed her mind. They were both exhausted and she hadn't the energy to face another confrontation with him.

Talk to him tomorrow, she told herself. We'll both be a bit calmer by then.

In the meantime, she'd have to think up some reason for him to give to the police.

Crossing to the window to draw the curtains, she stood looking out into the garden. The lights were still turned on by the pool but the area immediately in front of it, which earlier had been empty, was now busy with the dark silhouettes of men passing backwards and forwards in front of the naked figure of the naiad.

In the bushes to the right, where Teague had set up his equipment, the foliage was suddenly illuminated by a burst of bluish-white light from a photographer's flash.

There was an efficiency and purpose about the scene which alarmed her, especially about the stocky figure of the chief inspector who, at that moment, emerged from the shrubbery to walk slowly towards the centre of the activity where he paused under the lights, hands in pockets, to survey his surroundings with the air of a man who knew exactly what he was looking for.

Abruptly, Roz closed the curtains over the scene.

If Noel was guilty of Oliver Hampden's murder, then she didn't rate his chances very highly against a man like Finch.

8

It was gone three o'clock when Finch finally got home.

Letting himself into the house where he had lived alone since his widowed sister remarried, he was struck, as he always was, by its silence and impersonality. He occupied only part of it now, only the sitting-room, his bedroom, the bathroom and the kitchen. The rest of it was shut off although it was dusted and cleaned by a woman who came in twice a week. He rarely met her and they communicated mostly by terse little notes which they left for one other by the bread-bin.

She had been the day before and the kitchen looked even more unused and tidy, the sink wiped dry and the work tops gleaming.

Her note read: 'You're out of furniture polish so I've bought some – 89p.'

In case he forgot to leave the money in the morning, he laid a pound coin on the half-sheet of paper. Next week, when she called again, he'd find the change placed on top of the same note. If she thought about it, she might scrawl 'Thank you' on the bottom.

Having done that, he helped himself to a can of beer from the stock he kept in the fridge and went back into the hall where he switched on the answering machine.

There were three messages, one from his sister Dorothy asking him over for a meal the following week, although he doubted if he'd make it; another from an ex-colleague, a former inspector, now retired who, no doubt finding himself with too much spare time on his hands, wanted to meet him for a drink one evening.

The third was from Nina Gifford, speaking before the tone went so that he lost the first part of her message.

'... Danny. Sorry to bother you but could you ring me back as soon as you're in? I'm so worried about him.' There followed a pause before she added self-consciously, 'Thanks, Jack. 'Bye.'

The message referred to her younger brother with whom she shared a flat in London and who had been in and out of trouble as long as Finch had known him.

Well, it was too late to phone her now. He'd have to ring her in the morning.

He felt mildly exasperated by the call; not towards Nina herself but on account of her relationship with her brother. Why on earth didn't she kick him out? He was no bloody good and never would be although Finch could understand her need to hang on to him. She had no one else.

As for Nina herself, his feelings towards her were so complex that even he wasn't entirely sure exactly where he stood in his relationship with her. For that matter, she probably felt the same.

He had first met her several years before when he had been investigating the murder of an art dealer, Eustace Quinn, whose body had been found in one of the outbuildings at the house in Althorpe where she and Max Gifford were then living. He had been attracted to her at that first meeting; not that it had done him much good. She'd been too much in love with Max to pay any attention to him.

He had lost touch with her at the end of the investigation when she had sold the house and moved back to London after Max's death.

He hadn't seen her again until the previous summer when he had been involved in another murder inquiry at Selhaven, near the Essex coast, where she, too, had been staying for a few days.

It was one of those coincidences which, if he hadn't been a sceptic, he might have put down to fate taking a hand in his life.

The contact renewed, he had met her several times since then, always in London, either at her flat or for dinner in a restaurant although, despite a growing attachment on her part as well as his, the relationship hadn't progressed much further.

There were too many other emotions standing in the way, mostly her continuing love for Max which she'd never got over. Then there was his own guilt at the part he'd played in Max's death, however absurd such a feeling might be.

What bound them, he supposed wryly, was mutual loneliness and a shared involvement in a past murder case which was, when you came to consider it, a hell of a basis on which to form any relationship; friendship even, let alone anything more.

Switching off the answering machine, he tramped upstairs to bed, clutching in one hand the tin of beer, in the other the photostat of Roz Bennet's prompt copy of the play, *The Ingsby Inheritance*, the second act of which he intended reading before he went to sleep.

It was, of course, a love scene. Sod's law; it had to be.

Propped up on the pillows, he glanced at his watch before beginning to mouth the words half-aloud to himself, too tired to take in much of the meaning although here and there a piece of dialogue stood out on the printed page.

'I love you, Helena. I'd walk through fire for you.'

As he read, it struck him as ironic that Fielding who, according to Teague, had been in love with Annabel Thorpe before Hampden had started an affair with her, should have found himself playing opposite her in a scene in which he'd been obliged to speak these lines to her in public, in front of an audience of thirty people.

How had Fielding taken it? he wondered. And Annabel Thorpe, come to that?

At the end of the scene, he checked his watch again.

Teague had been right about the time it lasted. Allowing for pauses and a slower rate of delivery than his own reading speed, the action would have taken about twenty minutes to perform. Add on, say, another five minutes for the audience to be ushered out of the dining-room into the garden at the end of the first act, which was when Hampden had last been seen alive, and that gave the murderer almost half an hour.

Plenty of time.

And that wasn't all.

Switching off the bedside lamp, he lay in the dark, going over in his mind the other implications which his reading of the scene had raised.

First, Roz Bennet had misled him when she made her statement; deliberately, he suspected. She had said that Fielding made his exit at the end of the scene, which wasn't correct. He had left a good three minutes, possibly four, before its conclusion.

As for Annabel Thorpe, although she had remained on the set longer than Fielding, having had a short piece of dialogue to exchange with the butler, she, too, had left before the scene was finished; in her case, in the direction of the terrace, not the courtyard. According to Roz Bennet, Annabel Thorpe was supposed to remain there until it was time to make her entrance through the doors which led on to the stage at the beginning of the third act, when she would discover Lord Ingsby's body, seated at the desk, apparently shot through the heart.

In fact, the whole plot of the play was devised so that none of the characters had an alibi, leaving the audience guessing who had murdered Lord Ingsby until the final scene.

Given that premise, wasn't it possible that Hampden's murderer had been well aware of this and had made use of the plot when committing the real crime? It was even possible that the play had inspired the murder in the first place.

And that suggested that the murderer had been familiar with the play, which in turn could imply that it was someone closely connected with its production, not a casual visitor to the house such as a member of the audience or the catering staff.

Lying there and listening to the traffic in the distance, Finch caught a first glimpse into the mind of the murderer.

If he was right, then the killer had to be both intelligent and ingenious; someone who had grasped the possibilities the play offered to kill Hampden and had a strong enough motive for wanting him dead.

101

An opportunist, therefore, with a quick mind and a sense of humour; or at least a sardonic element in his or her make-up.

For there was an ironic twist to the fact that Hampden, the actual victim, should have been murdered at the point in the play when Lord Ingsby, the character he was playing and the fictional victim, was supposed to have met a similar fate.

But when exactly?

Humping over on his side, Finch stared at the curtained window round which faint streaks of orange light were filtering from the street lamps outside.

Hampden had last been seen alive by Roz Bennet at the end of the first act and discovered dead, also by her, at the end of the second.

He could have been killed at any time during that intervening half an hour or so while the scene by the pool was being acted out.

If it was during the scene, then Fielding and Annabel Thorpe could be eliminated. Both of them had taken part in it until a few minutes before its end and therefore had perfect alibis, supported by thirty witnesses.

That theory also took Christopher Hampden and Lady Kelling off the list. According to Hampden's preliminary statement, he'd spent most of the time with his mother in her sitting-room, leaving it only a few minutes before the scene was due to end although he'd have to get full statements from both of them tomorrow; correction – today; it was well past midnight.

Which left Mary Hogarth, Clayton and Wyvern in the running. And Roz Bennet and Teague as well. Both of them could have found the time while the scene was going on to slip into the dining-room, Roz Bennet through the hall, Teague via the terrace doors.

And that was another point to bear in mind. Just because the cord used to strangle Hampden had been taken from the terrace doors, it didn't necessarily mean the murderer had entered that way. There was the other entrance, the door at the far end of the dining-room which gave immediate access to the passage leading into the hall.

Not much in the way of motive against either Roz Bennet or Teague, though, which didn't mean one wouldn't turn up.

But supposing the murder had been committed towards the end of the scene, after Fielding and Annabel Thorpe had made their exits?

That let out Wyvern who was on the set but put Fielding and the Thorpe woman back into the picture, still leaving Mary Hogarth and Clayton on the list.

Not Teague, though, nor Roz Bennet. Both of them had alibis which covered their movements for those last minutes. Roz Bennet had been firing the prop gun out of the window while Teague had been busy at that console of his, lowering the lights and fading out the music as the scene ended.

It also meant Christopher Hampden was without an alibi. It was towards the end of the scene that he'd left his mother's sitting-room and had made his way to the Stone Gallery to speak to the catering manager, a route which would have taken him past the dining-room.

It also, Finch realized, left Lady Kelling alone and without an alibi either.

Half-asleep, he found the word 'infanticide' surfacing in his mind.

The murder of a son. Not a usual crime, especially when the child in question was in his forties and strongly built with it.

Infanticide. Matricide. Patricide. Fratricide.

Unlikely words, all of them, especially when taken as a group.

Odd that there wasn't one to cover the most common motive of all for murder – sexual passion; husbands who kill their wives, or lovers their mistresses. Or vice versa, come to that.

Amatricide?

The light seeping in round the curtains had begun to turn grey and somewhere out in the garden a bloody bird struck up the dawn chorus.

Dragging the pillow round his ears, Finch drifted off into an uneasy sleep.

9

The question of timing was one of the items which Finch stressed when, the following morning, he met the detectives assigned to the investigation for a briefing at Divisional Headquarters in Chelmsford before returning to Cressetts.

As he saw it, this aspect of the case was crucial; that, and how it applied to the group of immediate suspects.

For, as he listened to the reports of the CID officers, it became clear that, as he had suspected, unless any evidence turned up to the contrary, the members of the Cameron Club could be eliminated from the inquiry. According to the statements taken the previous evening, no one in the audience had been missing during the second act. All the same, to make quite sure he dispatched five of the plain-clothes men to the Crown Hotel in Widford for a final check before the party left later that day for Stratford-upon-Avon, the next stop on their tour.

The catering staff could also be eliminated on much the same grounds. All of them had remained in the Stone Gallery preparing for the buffet supper, and could alibi each other. Their statements also partly corroborated Christopher Hampden's account of his movements. He had indeed appeared in the gallery to speak to the catering manager and had remained for several minutes although no one had noticed the exact time when he arrived or how long precisely he had stayed. It was shortly after he had left that the staff had learned of Oliver Hampden's murder.

As for the domestic staff, there was only one who lived in,

Hampden's widowed housekeeper, a Mrs Franklin, who had been given the evening off and had chosen to visit her daughter in Widford rather than watch the play. Her alibi had been verified earlier that morning. Apart from her, there were a couple of local women who came in on a daily basis and had been at home with their families watching television at the time of the murder.

Which left only the actors on the list of suspects, together with Roz Bennet and Cliff Teague, who were familiar with the play and its timing, and Lady Kelling who, on her own admission, had retired to her room and had not joined the others in the garden.

This theory, which Finch had expounded that morning during the briefing, was evidently still on Boyce's mind when a little later the two of them set off by car for Cressetts.

'Someone who knew the play, yes. I'll grant you that,' the sergeant remarked with a magnanimous air. 'And the means were there. Any one of them could have got hold of that curtain cord. But it still doesn't go half-way to establishing a motive.'

Finch made an effort to rouse himself. His mind had been on Nina rather than the investigation.

Before setting out for headquarters that morning he had tried to phone her but there had been no answer. He had been too pressed for time to try again later and, once the conference had got under way, he had quite frankly forgotten all about her.

It was only when he was seated in the car on the way to Cressetts that he had the mental space to think about her, and remembered with a surge of guilt that he hadn't tried to ring her again.

He imagined her sitting by the phone, wondering why he hadn't got in touch with her.

Boyce's remarks about motive cut through his thoughts, bringing him back to the matter of the investigation which, in its turn, he had temporarily forgotten.

'There's Fielding for one,' he pointed out. 'According to Teague, Hampden had been having an affair with his girl friend, Annabel Thorpe. And what about her? Supposing Hampden had broken off the relationship? That'd give you jealousy and revenge which isn't bad for starters. Then there'd evidently been some row or other between Hampden and Clayton; God knows what about. We may find out when we interview Clayton. As for the others including Miss Bennet, it's too early to say. We'll need to dig about a bit more; see what we can turn up.'

They both fell silent, Boyce presumably mulling over the chief inspector's comments while Finch's own thoughts returned to Nina.

He'd have to find the time to ring her during the day and ask her what was the matter. He could only hope to God it wasn't anything too urgent. He had enough on his plate as it was without having to concern himself with Danny's problems.

Shortly afterwards they turned into the courtyard at Cressetts where Finch conferred briefly with Kyle and Barney who had arrived before them and whom he dispatched with their stop-watches and tapes to check on the exact distances Fielding and Annabel Thorpe would have had to cover and how long it would have taken them once they'd left the pool to reach the courtyard entrance and the terrace. McCullum and Bretherton went with them, Bretherton to video the scene in daylight, McCullum to take still shots.

Finch followed them as far as the archway leading into the garden where he halted to make his own survey of the setting.

The gilt chairs and the lighting stands were still in position, looking forlorn and incongruous in the sunlit garden like leftover decorations from a party.

And how silent it was!

Somewhere over to the right among the trees a wood pigeon called, softly voluptuous. Apart from that, there was no sound. Even the house seemed asleep as if under some enchantment.

He turned to look at it, seeing it in detail for the first time. Although he had little interest himself in material possessions, requiring only a few basic creature comforts, and very rarely begrudged other people theirs, he nevertheless felt a touch of envy towards Christopher Hampden who, on his brother's death, would presumably inherit all this.

Crossing the courtyard towards the front door, it occurred to him that, when it came to the matter of motive, that fact alone could have given Christopher Hampden a good enough reason for wanting his brother dead.

The front door was set open but the entrance hall was deserted; no sign of Hampden or anyone else come to that.

Well, Hampden could wait until later. It was Fielding's statement that the chief inspector wanted to hear first and, having installed himself once more in Oliver Hampden's office, he sent a uniformed man off to find him.

Noel was sitting in the buttery when the summons came. He had deliberately come down late for breakfast in order to avoid both Roz and Annabel, neither of whom he could bring himself to face. Annabel's defection was by far the worst but, as if it were some great, aching wound, he tried to minimize the pain of her betrayal by concentrating on the more recent sting of Roz's disloyalty.

How dare she accuse him of lack of initiative? Hadn't he got the bloody play off the ground in spite of all the problems he'd had to deal with? If that wasn't initiative, he'd like to know what the hell was.

Part of him, however, knew that she was right and this also rankled. He was no good at his job – that fact had to be faced – and the chances were that he'd get the push anyway, even though Oliver was dead.

As for Oliver's murder, his mind veered away from that. It was too awful to contemplate.

And what possible reason could he give to the chief inspector for having hung about near that archway after he'd come off from the second scene instead of going straight back to the house?

It was all very well Roz telling him to think of an answer. He'd done nothing else all night and still hadn't come up with a plausible excuse.

It was at this point that a uniformed constable had come to

107

fetch him and, getting to his feet, Noel followed the man along the passage to the office.

He entered the room reluctantly, seating himself in an upright chair which Finch had swivelled round to face the desk.

So the interview was going to be formal, Noel thought gloomily although he was a little cheered by the chief inspector's appearance. There was a pleasant, homely air about him, not at all intimidating, which Noel felt he might be able to use to his own advantage.

The interview began easily enough, Finch merely confirming a few basic facts which Fielding had given the previous evening to one of the CID officers.

Unmarried. Twenty-six. London address – number 17 Wimbourne Grove, NW6. Worked as a PR assistant in the firm Hampden and Brownlow.

'So Oliver Hampden was one of your bosses,' Finch remarked cheerfully. 'Easy to get on with, was he?'

'On the whole, yes,' Noel replied after a moment's pause which wasn't lost on the chief inspector.

Uncertain how much the police knew about the bollocking he'd got from Hampden over the Clayton business, not to mention the Annabel affair – and affair was the right word – Noel was unsure how frank he ought to be.

'We'd had our differences from time to time,' he added, hedging his bets, just in case Finch was acquainted with the facts. 'Nothing serious, though.'

'And I understand that you produced as well as acted in the play that Mr Hampden was putting on for the G. B. Russell centenary,' Finch continued, making a mental note of Fielding's equivocation.

Fielding immediately became more animated. 'Yes, that's right. Oliver especially asked me to take charge of the production. He'd seen a cabaret I'd organized for. . . .'

'It's the part you played in the second scene, the one that took place in the garden, that I'm interested in,' Finch said, cutting short Fielding's overeager explanation with a smile which was intended to be disarming. It was obvious Fielding would have to be kept to the point or they'd be there all morning.

Watching from across the width of Hampden's desk, Finch was struck by the man's stress. From the look of him, he hadn't slept the night before. His eyes were brilliant with exhaustion, giving his face a feverish animation which was at odds with the fixed weariness of the rest of his features.

It would be easy enough to crush him. He was half-way already to breaking down.

It was one of the reasons why Finch held back. The conquest would be too easy.

'Am I right in thinking,' he continued in the same relaxed and easy manner, 'that the scene lasted about twenty minutes and that you made your exit about four minutes before the end?'

Noel nodded miserably. He could anticipate the next question, for which he still hadn't thought up an adequate answer, but when it came it was almost a relief.

'What did you do after that, Mr Fielding?'

'I walked up the lawn towards the archway that leads into the courtyard. I – I stood there watching the rest of the scene.'

'Why?'

The simple interrogative was a lot less sharp than Roz's. It was almost apologetic in its persistence as if Finch regretted having to press the point.

'Well,' Noel began, casting round desperately, 'I wanted to see the audience's reaction to the prop gun being fired.' Even to him, it sounded plausible; in fact, not a bad piece of improvisation, given the circumstances. Warming to the idea, he went on, 'You see, the gun's supposed to be fired in the dining-room, not from the office window. I wondered if the audience would notice. As it happened, it went down pretty well, better than I'd hoped. Wyvern managed to direct their attention towards the terrace and I don't think it occurred to anyone that the shot hadn't come from the library at Highwood House; the dining-room, that is.'

It was a mistake, he realized, to have added that last remark.

109

It confused the explanation which, up to that point, had sounded reasonable, giving it a dying fall.

Finch, too, was aware of the lameness of Fielding's account, but not just its ending. The whole story was overelaborate and circumstantial.

All the same, he nodded encouragingly. 'Go on, Mr Fielding. What did you do next?'

'Well, I knew Wyvern had only a line to say after the gun was fired before he'd start leading the audience back into the house for the last act, so I thought I'd better make myself scarce.' Fielding paused and a look of genuine anguish passed across his face. 'When I went into the hall, there were several people milling about. Someone – I think it was Clayton – told me Oliver had been murdered. It was such a terrible shock. What with that and the general worry over the play, I suddenly felt awful and I had to rush out into the courtyard to throw up. I must admit I'd had a fair amount of champagne before the play started. And I hate anything to do with death!'

The last comment was made on a rising note which was close to panic.

'Thank you, Mr Fielding,' Finch said gravely. 'That's all I need for the time being. I shall have to have a written statement from you at some later stage.'

'You mean I can go?' Fielding sounded astonished and relieved that it was all over. Scrambling to his feet, he made a dash for the door like a schoolboy who, having been dismissed by the headmaster, expects any moment to be called back for a final punishment.

As he left, Finch turned to Boyce with a grin. 'We've got corroboration for at least a part of his statement. One of the uniformed men reported finding some vomit in a corner of the courtyard last night.'

The sergeant was less amused. 'You didn't ask him anything about the Thorpe woman.' He sounded accusatory.

'No, I didn't because I intend getting her side of the story first. We can always go back to Fielding later and clobber him with her statement if we have to. I'd rather leave him thinking he's been let off the hook; soften him up a bit. And I know

110

what you're going to say, Tom,' Finch went on as Boyce drew in a breath of protest. 'Fielding could have murdered Hampden. It wouldn't have taken him long to nip along from that archway to the dining-room without being seen. There's plenty of cover in the way of shrubs and bushes. And that's another reason why I want to interview Annabel Thorpe. According to Miss Bennet, she should have been waiting about on the terrace to make her entrance through those double doors for the third act. If that's where she was, no one, not even Fielding, could have got in that way.'

'That still doesn't clear him,' Boyce pointed out. 'There was nothing to stop him from entering through the house. It'd only be a matter of crossing the courtyard and letting himself in through the front door.'

'Risky, though. Fielding was taking part in that garden scene until a few minutes before the end. It wouldn't have given him long to commit the murder anyway. He'd know better than anyone else about the timing. He'd also know that, as soon as that prop gun was fired, Roz Bennet would leave the office and head for the dining-room to set the stage for the final act. But according to her, she didn't see Fielding when she crossed the hall, only Lady Kelling and Clayton who was standing on the front steps. God knows how long he was there; we'll have to check with him later. But if he was there any length of time, Fielding would have had to pass him.'

'I get your point,' Boyce conceded reluctantly.

'Then ask the PC on duty to wheel Miss Thorpe in and we'll hear her statement before we theorize any more on Fielding's movements.'

In the event, the interview with Annabel Thorpe had to be postponed.

Boyce had got to his feet and was half-way towards the door when someone knocked briskly and decisively on it, as if whoever was outside had every intention of being admitted.

On opening the door, the sergeant found Roz Bennet standing in the hall.

'May I come in?' she asked, looking past Boyce's shoulder and addressing Finch.

'Yes, of course,' Finch replied, showing no surprise as he got to his feet but wondering what on earth had brought her there. 'Sit down. And what,' he continued as she took the chair opposite him, 'can I do for you, Miss Bennet?'

Roz lifted her chin and took a deep breath, an old theatrical trick which relaxed the shoulder and stomach muscles. As for her lines, she had them rehearsed, having given them considerable thought since she had spoken to Noel the previous evening. The difficulty was to make them sound spontaneous.

And then she said to herself, Oh, what the hell. Finch and his sergeant aren't stupid. They're going to realize I must have thought about what I'm going to say.

She launched into the first part of her speech.

'There's a couple of points I wanted to add to my statement,' she announced.

'And what might those be?' Finch asked. He had assumed his avuncular expression, benign and attentive.

'The first's about Noel – Mr Fielding. I don't think I made it quite clear to you yesterday that I happened to notice him at the end of the scene by the pool.' Indicating the window facing her, she went on, 'As I told you, I was standing over there, watching the action so that I could follow the cues. After Noel came off, I saw him walk up the lawn and stand by the courtyard entrance. He was still there when I fired the prop gun out of the window. It was only a few seconds later that I left the office and went to the dining-room. He wasn't in the hall, so I assume he was still in the garden.'

She stopped there, leaving it to the chief inspector to draw his own conclusions – that Noel couldn't possibly have murdered Oliver Hampden. He simply wouldn't have had the time.

If Finch made the connection, he showed no sign.

All he said, his voice and expression non-committal, was, 'Thank you, Miss Bennet. My sergeant has made a note of what you've said. And your second point was what?'

Roz hesitated, genuinely at a loss this time as to how to begin. Although she had no qualms about lying on Noel's behalf, the other matter which she wanted to raise with the chief inspector troubled her more deeply and, for this reason, she had failed to think through exactly what to say, trusting to a last-minute inspiration to provide the right words.

But they had to be said. If Noel was to be protected, someone else had to be sacrificed. It was a small consolation that she would be telling Finch only what was the truth.

Her colour high, she began awkwardly. 'It's about Christie – Christopher Hampden. Yesterday afternoon, I met him in the garden and we got talking, mainly about Cressetts. I thought you ought to know that he's very fond of the place. From what he said, I had the impression that he'd like to own it.'

She broke off, conscience-stricken and unable to continue as she had intended with a more detailed account of Christie's plans for the place. Even the little she had said seemed a dreadful betrayal, not just of him and their private conversation but of the trust he had placed in her by speaking of those dreams which she knew he would confide to few other people.

Finch, damn him, remained inscrutable.

'Thank you, Miss Bennet,' he said politely. 'Is that all?'

'Yes,' Roz replied. She couldn't bring herself to add another word.

Straight-backed and with head held high, she made her exit.

As soon as the door closed behind her, Finch remarked, 'She's lying about Fielding. I checked that window last night and there's no way she could have seen anyone standing by that courtyard entrance without half-breaking her neck. Interesting, though, isn't it? Why should she want to give Fielding an alibi? Does she suspect he murdered Hampden? Or has he confessed to her and is she lying to protect him? Either way, it looks as if they've put their heads together and concocted a story between them.'

'Could be,' Boyce agreed. 'What about Christopher Hampden? Was she lying about him, too?'

'No; that sounded authentic to me; not that it was anything new. It's obvious he'd inherit the place if his brother died without heirs and that's a good enough motive in anybody's book. It could fit in with the timing of the murder as well.'

'I don't follow.'

'Look at it this way, Tom. According to Teague, Oliver Hampden was having an affair with Annabel Thorpe. Now that could give not only Fielding a motive for wanting him dead but Christopher Hampden as well. What if Hampden was thinking of marrying her? If he did and produced an heir, his younger brother's chances of inheriting the Russell estate would go out of the window. It's one of the themes of the play, incidentally – the question of inheritance – which could have given Christopher Hampden the idea in the first place. Supposing he chose this weekend to get rid of his brother? With a house full of people, it'd be difficult to check on his movements.'

'He's got an alibi of sorts,' Boyce pointed out.

'Which doesn't cover all of that second scene. Shortly before the prop gun was fired, he was in the gallery talking to the catering manager. He could easily have slipped into the dining-room on his way there and strangled his brother.'

'Do you want to interview him now?'

'No; we'll see Annabel Thorpe first; find out what she has to say about Fielding and Oliver Hampden and what she was doing after she made her exit.'

It was with quiet amusement that Finch observed the sergeant's reactions when, a few minutes later, PC Daventree showed her into the office.

Boyce, who had been sitting slumped in his chair, immediately sat upright and recrossed his legs.

Annabel Thorpe's movements were as contrived to gain attention; in her case, the chief inspector's. Boyce received not so much as a glance.

Moving with a languid elegance, as if exhausted by grief, she sat down opposite Finch, regarding him with a look of wide-eyed sincerity which challenged him to be hard on her.

She was certainly attractive; but calculating with it. Before he had a chance to open his mouth, she had begun her own emotional appeal, no doubt carefully considered, about how

114

appalling it was about poor Oliver and how dreadful she felt about his death.

'It may sound a terrible cliché, Chief Inspector, but we were such good friends,' she concluded.

'I think you and Mr Hampden were a little more than that,' Finch remarked, watching for her reaction. 'Weren't you lovers?'

'Oh, my God, who told you that?' she exclaimed. 'If it was Noel. . . . '

It was difficult to tell how far she was sincere although the remark about Fielding had the ring of real resentment.

'As a matter of fact, it wasn't Mr Fielding.' Finch had no intention of telling her it was Teague. 'But I gather the information is correct?'

'And none of your business,' she said sharply.

'No? I'm afraid in a murder inquiry it could well be, Miss Thorpe. What exactly was your relationship with Mr Hampden? Were you engaged? Was there any talk of marriage?'

'No; not so far.'

Which could only mean that she had hoped Hampden would propose to her. He'd be a catch for any woman; wealthy; the owner of Cressetts; joint managing director of a successful London firm. She'd be a fool not to raise her hopes and she certainly wasn't that.

'No quarrel?' he suggested.

She stared at him, trying to outface him, but Finch was well practised in that particular ploy and it was she who lowered her glance.

'No; quite the reverse. We were planning to spend a week in Cannes together in September.'

Nice work, although he only had her word for it.

'And Mr Fielding,' he continued. 'What was your relationship with him?'

She was intelligent enough to see the point and too shrewd not to turn it to her advantage.

'Whatever Noel may have told you to the contrary, we were merely friends; no, not even that; little more than acquaintances. I met him a few months ago at a party and he asked me, quite out of the blue, to take part in the Russell Festival. That's all.'

'Nothing more?'

'If you mean, were we lovers, then certainly not!' She seemed indignant that such a thought should cross the chief inspector's mind although there was a self-satisfied note in her voice when she added, 'I think Noel may have been infatuated with me but I can assure you it was all on his side. I did nothing to encourage him.'

Finch doubted the last part of her statement. She was the type of woman who would need the constant flattery of a man's attention and poor bloody Fielding had, it seemed, merely served as a stopgap until the more eligible Oliver Hampden had appeared on the scene.

He felt almost sorry for the man although that didn't prevent him from putting a mental cross against Fielding's name in the list of suspects. A motive had now been established.

Getting out the photostat of Roz Bennet's prompt copy of the play, he turned to the second act.

'According to the script, Miss Thorpe, you made your exit just before the end of the scene in the garden and you should have waited outside the terrace doors, ready to make your entrance at the beginning of the last act. Is that what you did?'

For the first time during the interview, she lost a little of her self-assurance. Her hands, which had been lying clasped loosely in her lap, began to stir and one went up in a defensive gesture to push back the wing of pale-gold hair.

'As a matter of fact, no,' she said. 'You see, I wanted to repair my make-up. Poor Noel had flung himself a little too enthusiastically into his part as my lover and I felt – well, rather rumpled after it. I knew I'd have plenty of time. It'd take ages for the audience to get back into the house for the last act. So I rushed off to do my face and hair.'

She smiled at Finch, inviting him to sympathize with her natural feminine desire to look her best.

His voice and expression perfectly bland, Finch asked, 'Where did you go, Miss Thorpe?'

'Oh, only round the corner of the house. There's a down-

116

stairs cloakroom with a mirror next door to G.B.'s study. I went in there. You can get to it from the outside. There's a vestibule with a door leading into the garden.'

It was only after Finch had thanked her and Boyce had escorted her out of the room that the chief inspector gave vent to his feelings.

'Blast her! You realize what she's done, Tom? Messed up part of my theory. While she was off doing her damned face, that door leading off the terrace on to the stage wasn't covered. Anyone, including Fielding, could easily have slipped in there and strangled Hampden.'

Boyce took the setback more sanguinely. 'D'you want to have a look at this cloakroom?'

'Later. I need to talk to Christopher Hampden. And Clayton. Let's try running Hampden to earth first.'

But Christopher Hampden still proved elusive.

On leaving the study, they were met in the hall by a haggard-faced Mary Hogarth who informed them that Christopher Hampden was in the middle of a series of important telephone calls to his brother's business associates and lawyers.

Could the interview be postponed for the time being?

Finch agreed reluctantly although he could understand that Hampden's death had left his brother with a great many loose ends to tie up.

'Tell him,' he said, 'that I'm off now to speak to Mr Clayton but I'll be back. I'd appreciate it if he could be free later this afternoon. I'd also like to speak to you as well.'

'Yes, of course,' Mary Hogarth said quietly, as she accompanied them to the front door. 'And I'll see Christie gets the message.'

As they stood on the steps while she gave them directions for finding where Clayton lived, an MG turned out of the courtyard and set off at too fast a speed down the broad beech drive in the direction of the village.

Hands in pockets, Finch watched it disappear from sight with a speculative gaze.

One – and possibly two – suspects were making their departure.

Well, let them go. If need be, he could always interview them again in London.

Which reminded him, he still hadn't phoned Nina.

10

There was a public phone box in the village and, telling Boyce to stop, Finch got out of the car and, shutting himself in the kiosk, put ten pence in the slot and dialled Nina's number.

He let it ring for nearly a minute, picturing to himself her flat in Swiss Cottage and the big, white sitting-room, dominated by Max Gifford's nude portrait of Lilith which hung above the shabby red chesterfield.

But there was no reply and eventually he hung up and retrieved his money.

'Something important?' Boyce asked nosily when the chief inspector returned to the car.

'My sister,' Finch lied. 'She wasn't in.'

Nobody, not even Dorothy and certainly not Boyce, knew about his relationship with Nina; not that he mistrusted Boyce's discretion. But there were certain areas of his private life which he confided to no one. Nina was one of them.

He comforted himself with the thought that whatever Nina had wanted to say to him about Danny, it couldn't be that urgent, otherwise she'd have waited in for his call.

Clayton's caravan was about a mile outside the village, parked in the corner of a field, a battered white Ford pick-up standing beside it. So the chances were the man was at home.

The five-barred gate leading into the field was closed and, rather than go to the trouble of opening it, Boyce drew the car up on the verge and the two men squeezed past the end of one of the upright posts. Judging by the gap between it and the hedge, this short-cut had already been well used by Clayton.

The caravan stood on an oblong of rough concrete which, together with a tap on the end of a length of stand-pipe and a washing-line slung between two poles, was the only concession, as far as Finch could see, to establishing a permanent site.

There was no attempt to create a garden, surprising when you considered that according to Teague this was Clayton's profession, and in places the surrounding grass had crept across the hard stand or grew between the cracks in long tufts.

The van itself had the same neglected air, its cream painted sides blotched with rust. A pair of crudely made wooden steps led up to the door which was set open.

As they approached, Clayton appeared in the doorway.

'Come about Hampden's death, have you?' he asked.

There was something about the man which Finch couldn't quite fathom. On the surface he seemed pleasant enough, with an expression of smiling frankness about the broad features which gave him an open, jovial air. And yet none of it added up. It was as if Clayton had prepared himself for this interview, smile and all.

He invited them inside willingly enough, apologizing as they entered for the state of the caravan.

Even to Finch's eyes, it was a mess. A pair of Wellington boots stood just inside the doorway; more clothes – working clobber by the look of them – were scattered about, while propped up in one corner was a collection of gardening tools among which, leaning casually beside the spades and forks, was a high-powered rifle.

A limp curtain, only half-drawn, partly closed off the far end of the caravan which formed a primitive kitchen. Through the gap, a two-burner camper stove was visible and a tiny sink let into a formica top, the surface of which was covered with dirty plates and mugs. Unwashed saucepans stood nearby on the floor.

There was no sign of a woman's presence and the state of the place suggested that Clayton was unmarried or divorced. It was unlikely he was widowed. He was too young; only in his mid-thirties.

Clayton cleared a couple of chairs for them by the simple method of tipping the clothes on them to the floor. He himself sat down on a couch which, judging by the pillow and the blanket bundled up together at one end, served at night as a bed.

It was Clayton who opened the interview, leaning forward with his elbows on his knees and looking at them directly from under sandy eyelashes with that honest-to-God expression of his.

'I suppose you want to know what I was doing when Hampden was murdered?' he said.

It was disarming. It also took some of the wind out of their own sails, giving Clayton the advantage, a fact which wasn't lost on the chief inspector.

He was a damned sight more intelligent than Finch had at first given him credit for, having taken him, along with his scruffy clothes, at face-value.

There was something else about him, too. He was enjoying the situation. Although he must have realized he was a suspect, it didn't seem to matter. To him, the interview was nothing more than a game.

It occurred to Finch that Clayton would fit his mental picture of the murderer – an opportunist with a warped sense of humour who had turned the fictional murder in the play into a real killing.

Using his official voice in an attempt to put the interview back on to a proper footing, Finch said, 'Yes; we'd like a statement from you, Mr Clayton, about your movements during the second scene. Where exactly were you?'

'Well now, let's think.'

Still smiling, Clayton leaned back and closed his eyes, making a pretence of trying to remember.

'I wasn't due on until the third act. After the audience had gone out into the garden, I hung about in the hall for a bit, say about a quarter of an hour, talking to Wyvern.'

'Did you see anybody else?' Boyce asked.

'Can't say I did,' Clayton replied and then waited, deliberately Finch suspected, until Boyce had made a note of his reply

121

before adding, 'Wait a minute, though! I tell a lie. I saw that dark-haired woman – what's 'er name? – the one who played the secretary, going up the stairs.'

'Mary Hogarth?'

'Yes; that's her. A bit later on, Wyvern went out into the courtyard, ready to make his entrance at the end of the second scene and soon afterwards I followed him as far as the porch to have a quick fag. While I was standing there, I heard the prop gun fired. A couple of seconds later, the Bennet woman came out of the office and went across the hall towards the dining-room. I don't know if she saw me. I'd finished my fag when she came running back and grabbed Christie Hampden who was coming out of the room where the party was going to be held. After that – well, all hell broke loose. From what she said, I gathered she'd found Hampden dead. Christie went rushing off to the dining-room and it was about then that the Fielding bloke came in and the audience started arriving. It was panic stations from then on. Christie came back and he and Wyvern got everyone into the gallery, me with them. I stayed there until your lot arrived.'

It was a comprehensive statement which, despite the casual nature of its delivery, covered all the facts, and for this reason Finch suspected that it had been carefully rehearsed along with Clayton's frank expression and too-ready smile. Underneath it, there also ran a challenge which was almost cocky in its self-assurance.

Go on; prove I'm lying, Clayton seemed to be saying.

And it would be difficult to prove he was, Finch realized. Up to a point, Clayton's statement was corroborated by Roz Bennet who had said she had seen him with Wyvern on her way to the office and again as she had left it to return to the dining-room when he had been standing on the porch steps, smoking a cigarette.

But the fact remained that there was an interval of about twenty minutes to fill and, in that time, Clayton could have had the opportunity to slip into the dining-room and strangle Hampden.

And according to Teague, Clayton had a motive.

This was an aspect of the case which Finch was inclined to leave to the end of the interview, using it as a final shot which he hoped would shake Clayton's complacency. For the moment, he preferred to concentrate on the events which had taken place immediately before the discovery of Hampden's body, especially those relating to Fielding's movements over which still hung a bloody big question mark.

Picking up on Clayton's earlier reference to Fielding, he remarked, 'Mr Fielding said that when he made his exit at the end of that second scene he stood in the garden by the court-yard entrance. Did you happen to notice him when you went out for your cigarette?'

'No; but I was standing just outside the front door. You can't see that archway properly from there. Fielding could have been there. On the other hand,' and here the jaunty grin again appeared on Clayton's face, 'he could've nipped round by the terrace and been doing Hampden in.'

Which was exactly what Finch was trying to check on, as Clayton damned well knew.

The man's smile was beginning to get on Finch's nerves. It was time, he decided, that it was wiped off.

He said abruptly, without bothering with any softening-up approach, 'I understand you had a quarrel with Mr Hampden a couple of years ago.'

The shot misfired. Clayton, who was handrolling a ciga-rette, prompted no doubt by his own remark that he had gone out into the courtyard for a smoke, looked up in the act of moistening the gummed edge of the flimsy paper oblong. He was not at all put out. In fact, he looked amused.

'Been listening to the gossip?' he asked.

Finch countered with a question of his own. 'What was the quarrel about?'

Clayton shrugged as he lit his cigarette. 'I used to work for Hampden as a contract gardener. He thought my work wasn't up to scratch so he gave me the push; got someone else in; not that it bothered me much. He was one of those blokes you couldn't satisfy. Nothing was ever right for him.'

It was said in an offhand, almost dismissive manner and yet

Finch wasn't entirely convinced. He could understand, however, why Hampden had got rid of the man. One glance around the caravan was enough to convince him that Clayton would be a careless employee, inclined to scant a job.

He'd have to check with Christopher Hampden exactly what had happened between Clayton and his brother and how serious the quarrel had been.

Clayton's answer raised another question which Finch now put to the man.

'But you took part in the play,' he pointed out.

Clayton grinned at him. 'Hampden didn't have much choice, did he? The bloke who should've played the part had to drop out at the last moment. Wyvern suggested I took it on. I'd done some acting in the past for the Widford Players and he thought I'd be all right. I was, too – all right, I mean. Anyway, there was no one else who was free, so I suppose Hampden had to put up with it. It was either me or scrapping the whole bloody play. Fielding came down from London and rehearsed me. He seemed satisfied and offered me the part.'

To Finch's mind, none of it quite added up. On the surface, the explanation sounded plausible enough but it left too many questions unanswered.

Had Hampden's response been as Clayton had described it? And why, if Hampden had dismissed him, had Clayton apparently been so willing to accept a role in the play which would bring him into close proximity with his ex-employer? Wouldn't it have been more natural under the circumstances for Clayton to refuse to help Hampden out of his dilemma?

These also were aspects of the case he'd have to discuss with Christopher Hampden, Finch decided.

He had one parting shot left in his locker which he prepared to fire as he got to his feet.

'Got a licence for that gun, have you?' he asked, nodding across to the corner of the caravan where the rifle was propped up among the gardening tools.

'Yeah, I have,' Clayton said. 'God knows where it is, though.'

'I'd like to see it,' Finch said in his official voice.

'What, now?'

'Yes; now, Mr Clayton.'

It cheered him up considerably to see the grin disappear from the man's face as, with bad grace, Clayton heaved himself to his feet and went through to the kitchen end of the caravan where he began rummaging among a heap of papers stuffed into a drawer.

Finch took the opportunity while Clayton's back was turned to exchange a grin of his own with Boyce.

When Clayton at last returned with the crumpled licence, Finch deliberately took his time examining it. It was in order, made out in Clayton's name; nothing to quibble over there.

All the same, he couldn't resist remarking as he handed the licence back, 'A .223 Ruger, I see. That's a powerful weapon, Mr Clayton. What do you use it for?'

'Rats,' Clayton said. He had recovered some of his former assurance although not quite all of it. The smile hadn't returned and his eyes, under his stubby lashes, were watching the chief inspector's face warily. As if conscious of this himself, he went on in a more expansive manner, 'I got a contract a few years back to clear some wasteland. There was a couple of old sheds on it which were overrun with rats; big 'uns, some of them. That's when I bought the gun, to sort the buggers out.'

The swear word seemed once more to re-establish that air of amused assurance which had so exasperated the chief inspector earlier in the interview.

But there was nothing much Finch could do about it except report Clayton's carelessness to the local police and, as he turned towards the door, he remarked, 'You realize it's an offence to have a firearm lying about like that? It ought to be locked up in a proper gun-safe.'

'OK; I'll see it's put away,' Clayton replied, following them to the top of the steps where he paused, his hands stuffed into the pockets of his jeans.

'Oh, by the way,' he added, as if the thought had just occurred to him, 'I forgot to mention I saw Hampden during that second scene.'

Finch halted, nonplussed for a moment. 'You mean Christopher Hampden?'

'No, Oliver; the boss.'

With Boyce behind him, Finch shouldered his way back into the caravan, forcing Clayton to retreat.

'Why the hell didn't you tell me that before?' he demanded, letting his anger show.

Clayton shrugged, apparently unconcerned although he was careful to keep the smile off his face.

'It didn't seem all that important,' he said.

He was aware that he had gone too far for he took another step backwards, putting more space between himself and the chief inspector.

'For God's sake, man, this is a murder inquiry not a bloody game!' Finch told him.

'Yeah,' Clayton conceded and added belatedly, 'sorry.'

'When did you see Hampden?' Finch asked, ignoring the apology. 'And I ought to warn you, Mr Clayton, that I want a straight answer. If there's any more mucking about, I'll have you down at Divisional Headquarters so fast your feet won't touch the ground.'

'Right. Well, let's see. It must have been towards the end of the second act, just after Wyvern went into the courtyard, like I said. While he was out there, I nipped along to the dining-room and stuck my head round the door.'

'Why?'

The question seemed to take Clayton off-guard. 'I dunno. Something to do, I suppose. I was a bit fed up hanging about in the hall and I wanted to check everything was OK for the last act.'

That wasn't the reason, although Finch found it impossible to guess what had been going on in Clayton's mind at the time; that is, if he was telling the truth in the first place although, on balance, he was inclined to believe him.

The man wasn't stupid. By admitting he'd seen Hampden, he must have realized he'd given himself the opportunity to commit the murder. And why do that, unless he was telling the truth?

126

'Go on,' Finch said. 'What was Hampden doing?'

'Nothing much: just standing about on the stage. He'd changed into the bloodstained shirt, the one he was supposed to wear in the last act.'

'Just a minute,' Boyce put in, his voice heavy with suspicion. He had taken out his notebook again and was standing, pencil poised over the page. 'Miss Bennet said in her statement that the curtains on the front of the stage were closed when she went back to the dining-room and found Hampden's body.'

It was a good point and Finch looked at Clayton closely to observe his reactions.

The man seemed unperturbed. 'Then he must have opened them, mustn't he and whoever killed him closed them again later? They weren't properly drawn back, only half-way. Perhaps Hampden wanted a bit more air. It was bloody hot on that stage with the lights on. I'd've done the same if I'd've been him.'

'Did he see you?' Finch asked.

'I don't think so. I told you, I only stuck my head round the door. I wasn't there for more than a couple of seconds. Then I went back to the hall and decided to have a fag on the front steps. Just as I got out there, I saw Wyvern disappearing through the archway, off to make his entrance, so I couldn't have been gone long. Soon after that, I heard the prop gun fired.'

'Is that the lot, Mr Clayton?' Finch asked. 'You're not going to think of something else to add to your statement later?'

Although the remark was made in the chief inspector's non-committal, professional voice, the sarcasm wasn't lost on Clayton who grinned a little ruefully.

'No; that's everything.'

'Only we'll need a written statement from you at some point,' Finch continued, 'as well as your fingerprints. And let me give you another warning. Wasting police time is a serious charge.'

Even that threat failed to ruffle the man.

127

'Right-oh,' he said cheerfully. 'I'll sign a statement whenever you like. You're the governor.'

Finch contained his anger until he and Boyce returned to the car. Climbing into the passenger seat, he slammed the door viciously behind him.

'You realize what this means, Tom? If Clayton's telling the truth, it messes up the whole bloody timing. Hampden must have been alive during most of that second scene which lets out both Teague and Wyvern who were on the set by the pool when that prop gun was fired.'

'But not the others,' Boyce said. He had already grasped the significance of Clayton's evidence and the remark was made as a statement rather than a question.

'No,' Finch agreed. 'Not Fielding or even Annabel Thorpe. How long would it take to strangle a man? A couple of minutes? I reckon that's all it would need; less time than it took Clayton to smoke his cigarette.'

11

By the time Finch and Boyce returned to Cressetts, the men had finished with the area round the pool and the chief inspector sent Kyle and some of the other CID men off to make a search of the courtyard and the terrace outside the dining-room.

In the first instance, he knew what they ought to find – the butt of Clayton's cigarette, which should be conspicuous. It was unlikely that any of the Hampden family or their guests would handroll their own.

As for the terrace, it was more a case of clutching at straws. He hardly expected them to come up with a button or a handkerchief which would give a clue to the murderer's identity.

It was more than likely, he thought, that the killer had entered the dining-room by that route and this theory included Annabel Thorpe, in spite of her statement that she'd been in the downstairs cloakroom, repairing her make-up at the crucial time. It was a less public means of entry than the door leading off the hall as it was poorly lit and partly screened from the rest of the garden by shrubbery. Besides, it gave the murderer immediate access to the stage where, if Clayton was to be believed, Hampden was standing, still alive, a mere few minutes before the end of the second act.

In his reading of the play the night before, he had included the first few pages of the last act, mainly to check who would have made an early entrance and would therefore have been waiting somewhere near the dining-room, ready to come on

129

stage. Annabel Thorpe was first, closely followed by Wyvern, then Mary Hogarth and Clayton. Christopher Hampden's entrance was delayed until the end of the scene.

Teague would have had to be on the set early as well, to take charge of the lighting and sound effects for the last act. But, as Finch had pointed out to Boyce, now that the time of the murder was narrowed down to the few minutes before the third act was due to begin, neither Teague nor Wyvern would have had the opportunity. Both of them were occupied with the scene in the garden.

However, the stage directions for the third act, printed in Roz Bennet's copy of the play, gave a clear picture of what Hampden himself must have been doing while that second act was being played out by the pool.

They read: 'Curtain up. Lord Ingsby is seated at the desk, facing the audience, his head thrown back and the front of his bloodstained shirt clearly visible. The blackmail letters are scattered on the floor beside him. The gun is also on the floor by his right hand.'

Hampden had clearly changed into the bloodstained shirt. But supposing he'd also taken up his position at the desk, ready for the beginning of the third act?

It was possible. He'd only have a few minutes before the opening of the third act. And, come to that, only a few more minutes to live.

And according to Pardoe, he'd been murdered while he was sitting down.

Seated like that, with his head back, Hampden would have been a perfect target for anyone coming in behind him through the terrace doors.

How many paces was it? He'd have to check but it couldn't be much more than four; easy enough, especially if the murderer was one of the other actors with a plausible excuse for being there, such as 'I thought I'd let you know that the second act is almost finished.'

Finch pondered the question as he crossed the courtyard towards the house. It was certainly feasible and it made sense of the fact that Hampden hadn't put up a struggle. He hadn't had the chance; he was a sitting duck.

The front door was closed on this occasion and he had to ring the bell, hoping that Christopher Hampden would answer it. Apart from getting a more detailed statement from the man, there were several specific points he wanted to put to him regarding the play in the light of this theory as well as the queries arising from his interview with Clayton.

But it was Mary Hogarth who let them in. Mr Hampden, she explained, was still busy on the phone.

'In that case,' Finch said pleasantly, opening the door into the office, 'perhaps you wouldn't mind answering a few questions yourself.'

She followed him into the room and sat down on the chair he indicated. As she settled herself, Finch made his own quick estimation of her.

Attractive. Or had been. Still striking-looking with all that dark hair. But something deeply unhappy about her. It was evident in her eyes. And she was much too tense.

In view of this, he began easily, taking her first of all through her connection with the Hampdens.

She had, it seemed, known the family for several years, ever since Oliver Hampden had asked her to set up a display of G. B. Russell's books in the bookshop she ran in Widford when they were first reissued in paperback. This had led to her being asked to edit the quarterly magazine for the Cameron Club, the Russell fan society.

'So you knew Oliver Hampden quite well?' Finch suggested casually. 'Got on with him, did you?'

When she replied, her voice was flat, almost toneless. 'Yes; it was a pleasure to work with him.'

She might have been able to control her voice but not her eyes. As she finished speaking, she lifted her glance and the expression in it was haunted with God knows what – a mute appeal to Finch not to continue with this line of questioning, a dreadful longing, a deep and tragic sense of loss.

For a moment, it took the chief inspector aback and then it was gone.

131

On a conscious level, he was aware of her answers as he took her through the next part of the interview, the role she had played in *The Ingsby Inheritance*, mentally noting her answers. On another level, his mind was occupied with interpreting that glance which Boyce, head bent over his notebook, had probably not seen.

The thoughts ran through his head in short disjointed sentences.

She had been in love with Oliver Hampden. Obvious. Had there been an affair? Possibly. But it was almost certainly unhappy. Rejected? Also possible. In which case, she'd have a motive. But what about opportunity?

Out loud, he said, 'Tell me, Miss Hogarth, where exactly were you between the end of the first act and the beginning of the third?'

Roz Bennet hadn't seen her on either of the two occasions when she'd crossed the hall, going to and returning from the office.

'I was sitting at the top of the stairs,' she replied.

Finch got up from his chair. 'Show me.'

She led the way into the hall and pointed up the staircase. 'Up there,' she explained. 'There's an armchair on the landing. I wanted to look over my lines. Roz – Miss Bennet – had to prompt me a couple of times in the first act. I was worried I might dry up.'

At least part of her statement was corroborated by Clayton who had said he'd seen her going up the stairs while he was standing in the hall talking to Wyvern.

Boyce said, 'See anybody crossing the hall?'

'No; but I wasn't particularly looking. I knew I'd hear the gun being fired and Roz coming out of the office, so I'd be warned when the second act was coming to an end. I was going to come down once the audience was back in the dining-room and wait in the hall until it was time to make my entrance in the third act.'

The explanation sounded reasonable and might very well be true.

Finch tested it out, going half-way up the stairs to a point where he could see the upper gallery. It broadened out into a wide landing where an armchair was standing, well back from the head of the stairs. Anyone sitting there would not only be out of sight from the hall but wouldn't have a clear view down the stairs either.

Coming down the steps, he said, 'There's a cloakroom, I believe, somewhere near the dining-room. Could you show me where it is?'

This time, she led the way along the passage to a point where it made a sharp right-hand turn. Here, in the angle, a small inner vestibule opened out, with a glazed door leading on to the terrace.

Mary Hogarth pointed to another door on the left. 'The cloakroom's there.'

'And Lady Kelling's sitting-room is where?'

'It's the room next door.'

'That's all,' Finch told her. 'Thank you for your help. If you see Mr Christopher Hampden, would you tell him I'd like to speak to him?'

He waited until she had turned the corner of the corridor before he opened the cloakroom door and stuck his head round it; not that there was much to see, only a lavatory and a wash-hand basin with a mirror on the wall above it.

Shutting the door, he let himself out of the other into the garden, beckoning to Boyce with his head to follow.

Once outside, he said in a low voice, 'She was in love with Oliver Hampden.'

'Was she?' Boyce sounded sceptical. 'What gave you that idea?'

'Take my word for it,' Finch replied over his shoulder. He had strolled off to the end of the terrace where, like the corridor inside the house, it took a sharp turn before continuing along the side of the other wing of the house in the direction of the dining-room.

At that point, the stretch of lawn leading down to the pool could be seen, also two of the pairs of doors leading into the dining-room. Outside the third, a piece of scenery depicting part of the interior of Highwood House was still propped up, only its unpainted back visible with its supporting struts.

'What do you think, Tom? If Annabel Thorpe's speaking the truth, she could've easily nipped along here to that cloak-room. Once round the corner of the house, she'd be out of sight of anyone in the garden.'

'Could be,' Boyce replied. 'I don't reckon much to her anyway as a suspect. Not enough motive.'

Finch let it pass. He had his own ideas about Annabel Thorpe which, for the time being, he wasn't prepared to argue over with the sergeant.

Instead, he turned back and re-entered the house through the vestibule door, remarking, 'If Hampden's still busy, let's see if we can find Lady Kelling. It's time we had a chat with her.'

As luck had it, they met Christopher Hampden, who was on the point of entering his mother's room and greeted them with the words, 'Ah, Chief Inspector! Mary said you were looking for me. Sorry I've been so tied up. Oliver's death has meant dozens of phone calls. Do you want to speak to me now?'

He sounded harassed but not really contrite, as if whatever business affairs had been occupying him took precedence over the chief inspector's inquiries, an attitude which exasperated Finch although he said mildly enough, 'As a matter of fact, I was hoping to interview your mother.'

'Well, then, come in!' Hampden threw open the door and led the way into a pleasant, sunny room, furnished with chintz-covered armchairs and with a great many ornaments in the way of porcelain figurines standing about on the mantelpiece and on several small tables.

In the middle of all this flowery femininity, Lady Kelling struck a more sombre note. Dressed in black, she sat in a straight-backed chair by the open window, her own spine as rigid as the chair itself. Her white hair and her blue eyes were the only bright features to relieve the severity of her appearance. A silver-knobbed cane was propped up beside her; her hands rested, clasped together, in her black silk lap.

134

She raised one of them to shake with the chief inspector when Hampden introduced him. It lay light and dry, like a dead leaf, in his own. Apart from this one gesture, she remained immobile, listening in silence while he expressed his regrets at her son's death.

It was an embarrassing moment, which Hampden seemed aware of for he asked the chief inspector, 'Do you want me to leave?'

'You can stay if you prefer,' Finch replied.

There was no point in interviewing them separately. He already had their preliminary statements, Hampden's which he'd taken himself and Lady Kelling's which Barney had noted down. Since then, they'd had plenty of time to concoct a story between them, if that's what they'd done, and seeing them together might give him an indication of any collusion. It wouldn't take much – an exchange of glances, an over-readiness to agree with one another.

He began with Lady Kelling. 'I understand you didn't go out with the others to watch the scene in the garden. You stayed behind in the house. Where exactly?'

'I waited in here,' Lady Kelling replied. 'I have difficulty walking any distance. Besides, I had very little interest in the play. It was Oliver's idea. I disapproved of it.' It was said in a clipped, decisive tone. 'In my opinion, it caused a great deal of unnecessary disruption. Those people,' and Finch assumed she was referring to the members of the Cameron Club, 'would have been perfectly well satisfied with a reception on the lawn. But Oliver insisted.' Fixing Finch with an intense gaze which challenged him to show any sympathy, she continued, 'I am too old, Chief Inspector, to wish to have my routine turned upside-down and my home invaded by a crowd of strangers.'

Hampden, who seemed both amused and embarrassed by his mother's outspokenness, said in explanation, 'Oliver only came down here occasionally at weekends. He had a flat in London, in the Barbican. My mother was in charge of the place while he was away.'

Now that Hampden had introduced himself into the

135

conversation, it seemed a good point at which to include him in the interview.

'You said you were here with your mother for most of the time during that second scene?'

'That's right,' Hampden replied, without so much as a glance in his mother's direction. 'As I told you last night, I left about five minutes before the scene was due to end to speak to the catering manager. Oliver had asked me earlier to make sure everything was ready for the buffet supper after the play.'

'How long were you there?'

'I've no idea. Only a few minutes.'

'Did you pass anyone in the hall on your way to the gallery?'

'No; not that I expected to. Annabel and Noel would have been out by the pool anyway. Teague as well. Roz was in the office. As for the others, I assumed they'd cleared off somewhere. Oliver had warned everyone to keep out of sight when the audience came back into the house for the last act. He said it'd spoil the illusion if they were seen hanging about, waiting to make their entrances.'

'Miss Hogarth said she was sitting at the top of the stairs. Did you happen to notice her?'

'No; but I wasn't particularly looking.'

'Or Clayton?'

'Oh, yes! I remember now. He was just going out of the front door as I came through the hall.'

It corroborated Clayton's statement but didn't clear Hampden. If Clayton had been telling the truth when he'd said he'd seen Hampden alive shortly before going out on to the steps for a cigarette, then Christopher Hampden would have had the opportunity to murder his brother on his way from his mother's sitting-room to the Stone Gallery.

It seemed to Finch a good moment in which to drop the first of his stones into the pond and see what ripples it created.

'About Clayton – I understand from him that he used to work here as a contract gardener but your brother dismissed him because his work was unsatisfactory. Is that right?'

It caused fewer waves than he had hoped; no sudden

consternation; no exchange of glances between Hampden and his mother. If they had got their heads together over the Clayton affair, it was difficult to tell. They were both remarkably self-controlled.

It was Lady Kelling who answered. 'Oliver terminated the contract with Mr Clayton about two years ago for the reason you suggested. His work wasn't up to standard.'

'And yet Clayton took part in the play.'

'There was very little choice, Chief Inspector. The actor who should have taken the role had to withdraw at the last moment. Mr Wyvern suggested Clayton as a replacement.'

'Wasn't it a bit embarrassing under the circumstances?'

There was a slight pause before Lady Kelling replied, her voice abrupt, 'Oliver was hardly likely to be embarrassed in his own house. As for Mr Clayton, I have no idea what his feelings about it were, although, as he agreed to take over the role, I can only assume he bore no grudge against Oliver.'

She's covering something up, Finch thought, but before he could press the matter further, Lady Kelling forestalled him.

'Since you're inquiring into my son's relationships with those who took part in the play, let me save you yourself some embarrassment, Chief Inspector, by confirming that, yes, Oliver was having an affair with Miss Thorpe, both here and in London although I have no idea what his intentions were towards her. I doubt very much that they included marriage. As to whether or not Miss Thorpe was aware of this, I suggest you ask her yourself.'

'I've already done so,' Finch told her.

He felt exasperated by Lady Kelling's assumption of control over the interview and at his own stupidity in allowing it to happen. She had effectively deflected the second stone, Annabel Thorpe, he had intended lobbing at her of much of its effect.

But he had established something worth knowing during that little exchange: Lady Kelling had disapproved of her elder son's relationship with Annabel Thorpe as much as she did of the play. And he was still left with one more throw to make.

He made it now.

137

'And Miss Hogarth?' he asked. 'What was Mr Hampden's relationship with her?'

He had hit his mark. For a long moment, Lady Kelling regarded him with distaste before turning to her younger son as if inviting him to deal with this unpleasant question which the chief inspector had been ill-mannered enough to raise.

Hampden said, 'My brother had no relationship at all with Mary Hogarth, apart from co-operating with her over the play and the Cameron Club magazine. She may have been fond of him. As I've never discussed it with her, I'm in no position to give an opinion.'

Which was no answer at all although, as Finch got to his feet, he was damned sure that both Christopher Hampden and Lady Kelling had been well aware of Mary Hogarth's feelings for Oliver Hampden but, for reasons of their own, had preferred to ignore them.

Was she another source of embarrassment like Clayton? he wondered. Someone who must not be discussed with strangers, not even the police who were investigating Hampden's murder?

He said, addressing Hampden, 'If you wouldn't mind coming with me to the dining-room, Mr Hampden, there's a detail about the staging of the play that I'd like to discuss with you.' Turning to Lady Kelling, he added, 'Thank you for your help.'

She declined to answer, merely making a curt little gesture of the head to indicate she'd heard him.

Outside in the corridor, Hampden gave Finch an oblique glance, half-humorous, half-apologetic, but he made no reference to the interview. Finch had suggested they go to the dining-room partly because he hoped that once they were alone Hampden might volunteer more information than he had done in his mother's company.

In the end, it was Finch who had to make the approach. 'Any idea where I might find Mr Teague?'

He ought to interview the man again anyway. At the same time, he intended asking him a few more questions about Clayton. If Lady Kelling and Hampden weren't willing to come clean, then Teague might be prepared to gossip.

'Sorry,' Hampden said. 'I think he's gone into Widford for a spare part for the motor mower. Is it anything important?'

'I was going to tell him he could move his equipment from the garden,' Finch replied, which was partly the truth. He had intended giving Teague this permission when he spoke to him.

'I'll pass the message on,' Hampden told him.

They had reached the dining-room and Hampden led the way in.

On Finch's orders, the stage had not yet been cleared and the set for the play remained in place, although the gilt chairs had been removed from the temporary auditorium.

Accompanied by Boyce, the chief inspector followed Hampden to the far end where they mounted the two steps on to the dais.

Here Hampden halted.

'What was it you wanted to know?' he asked. He had lost some of his self-assurance and was glancing uneasily about at the scenery and the props as if they reminded him too vividly of the last time he had stood in that setting.

Finch said, 'Your brother was sitting in that chair behind the desk just before the third act was due to begin. My sergeant's going to take up a similar position. All you have to do, Mr Hampden, is tell him if he's got it more or less right.'

Looking self-conscious, Boyce lowered his bulk into the chair and leaned backwards, arms dangling, head thrown back to expose the throat while the two men stood watching, Hampden with a look of horrified awareness, Finch with a detached and critical gaze.

'Well?' he asked.

'For God's sake!' Hampden protested.

'Is that roughly the right position?'

'Yes! And can we leave it there, please? I find all this very distressing.'

Good! Finch thought. It was part of his intention to get Hampden rattled. And while he'd got the man off guard, he might as well press home the advantage.

'Tell me, Mr Hampden,' he said, as Boyce got up from the

139

chair, 'who'll inherit Cressetts now that your brother's dead?'

'I will,' Hampden replied. 'But if you think. . . .'

Finch cut him short. Hampden might be the new owner but here in this room, at the scene of the murder, the chief inspector was still in charge if only temporarily.

'Thank you,' he said. 'That's all for now, Mr Hampden. I shall need to interview you again, probably tomorrow. Would you please make sure you're available?'

'Let him stew for a bit,' Finch told Boyce, as Hampden left the room.

'You reckon he's in the running?'

'Could be,' Finch replied. He was measuring the distance between the terrace doors and the chair. He made it five normal paces. 'He has motive and the means were here.' He indicated the brass hook where the curtain cord had once hung. 'And opportunity. There was time for him to stop off here after he left his mother's sitting-room to talk to the catering manager. And one thing's damned sure. Neither Hampden nor his mother is coming clean about Clayton. Something's going on there and I intend finding out what it is.' He glanced at his watch before adding, 'Come on, Tom. There's no point in hanging about here, waiting for Teague. I've got a briefing set up. If we push off now, there'll be time to stop off on the way for a pork pie and a beer.'

The second briefing took place later that afternoon at six o'clock at Divisional Headquarters where he first put out a press release, leaving it to Hapgood, the press officer, to face the journalists and TV crews. Oliver Hampden's murder had caused quite a stir, not only locally but also in London.

That done, he moved into the briefing room for the reports from the teams of detectives who had been engaged on that day's inquiries.

Much of it was negative. Barney's group, which had been checking with the members of the Cameron Club and the catering staff, hadn't come up with anything vital. The members of the club, who had since left Widford by coach for Stratford-upon-Avon, were able to alibi one another. No one had been missing from the audience when it left the dining-room to reassemble in the garden and no one had seen or heard anything unusual.

The same applied to the catering staff. All of them had remained in the Stone Gallery and could vouch for one another's presence there. However, they could remember Christopher Hampden coming into the room and speaking to the manager, which corroborated his statement but didn't take him off the list of suspects.

As for the driver of the coach, another long shot, he'd spent the evening in the local pub, playing darts.

Kyle and Barney's reports had a little more meat on them. The distances from the pool to the terrace and the courtyard entrance were respectively seventy and ninety-five yards, and would have taken someone walking at a normal pace just under one minute and one minute fifteen seconds to cover; or less if they'd hurried.

There was another negative on the search of the terrace although Kyle had found the butt of a handrolled cigarette on one of the front steps; this corroborated Clayton's statement, as Finch pointed out to Boyce as the briefing broke up, but did nothing to substantiate his claim that he had seen Hampden alive shortly before the end of the second act.

It was then well past nine o'clock and Finch had taken himself off to his own office where Boyce had followed him and seemed inclined to linger.

Finch wished to God he'd go home.

He wanted to try phoning Nina again which he couldn't do with Boyce hanging about. Besides, he would have welcomed a half-hour or so on his own, simply to think through the case and get his ideas down on paper, something else he was reluctant to do in front of the sergeant.

But as Boyce showed no signs of leaving, Finch finally capitulated and took a sheet of A4 paper out of his drawer, hoping that if he looked preoccupied, Boyce would finally take the hint and go home.

He was hopeless at drawing and the rough plan he sketched out of the house and gardens at Cressetts bore very little resemblance to reality.

Rather than being deterred, Boyce seemed interested in what the chief inspector was doing and came behind the desk to look over his shoulder.

Trust him to make some critical comment.

'The scale's all wrong,' he remarked.

'I know that,' Finch snapped back.

'So what's it in aid of?'

It should have been bloody obvious. 'I'm marking in where everybody was, or said they were, at the time Hampden was strangled.'

Boyce leaned down to look as Finch's biro marked in the crosses and initialled them, N.F. for Noel Fielding by the courtyard entrance, M.H. at the head of the stairs, A.T. in the downstairs cloakroom next to Russell's study. Finch could hear him breathing heavily close to his ear.

'And Professor Plum in the library,' Boyce remarked with a grin, and with that parting shot he left – thank the Lord.

As soon as he had gone, Finch reached for the phone.

Nina picked up the receiver so quickly that Finch suspected she must have been sitting over it, waiting for it to ring.

She said, 'Oh, thank God, you've phoned, Jack. I've been hoping you'd call.'

Finch tried to explain that he'd tried to get in touch with her earlier but she hurried on. He could hear the tension in her voice.

'It's Danny. He's supposed to be in Birmingham working. God knows what he's been up to, though. The police have been round here looking for him.'

'Did they say what they wanted him for?' he asked, keeping his own voice easy and matter-of-fact in order to calm her down.

'Not exactly but they asked if he was on drugs. I said not as far as I knew.'

Christ! Finch thought. That's all either of us needs.

He glanced at his watch. It was twenty to ten. The roads should be relatively empty. If he got a move on, he could be with her in little over an hour.

'Stay there,' he told her. 'I'm coming over.'

12

The turning where she lived, Harlow Gardens, was off Finchley Road and was lined with gaunt Victorian houses, divided up into bed-sits and flats. Like the others, hers, number seven, was large and ugly, constructed of dark brick and slate with jutting gables which gave the house a look of scowling intensity.

When he had first visited her there, he could not understand why, after Max's death and the sale of Althorpe House, she had chosen this place to live out of everywhere else.

Parking the car, he mounted the steps to the front door where he rang the bell for her first-floor flat.

Nina's voice, tinny and breathless, came crackling through the entry-phone speaker. 'Jack?'

Almost before he had time to answer, the buzzer sounded as the lock on the door was released.

She was waiting for him on the landing, hands outstretched, not to embrace him as he first thought but to bundle him inside as quickly as she could, although, once they were standing in the narrow hall, squashed together in close proximity, she brushed her cheek against his.

'Thank God you've come. I've been so worried.'

Not on his account, Finch thought wryly. Her concern was entirely for Danny.

All the same, he felt the need to apologize. 'Sorry, I couldn't make it sooner. There was a traffic hold-up on the motorway. . . . '

She wasn't listening. Leading the way into the sitting-room,

143

she was saying over her shoulder, 'Come in and sit down. Coffee? It's made. I've only got to heat it up.'

'Yes, coffee would be. . . . '

But she had already gone, disappearing into the kitchen to fetch the tray, leaving him alone in the room.

He remained standing for several moments, reminding himself of the setting in which Nina now lived.

It was a large room, furnished with the pieces he remembered from the house in Althorpe which was where he'd first met her. Max, too. And Danny.

There were changes since he had last been here. The huge, nude portrait of Lilith which had once hung above the chesterfield was gone. The curtains, too, were drawn over the windows which, in daytime, looked out over a garden full of trees, which was probably why she had bought the flat. It must have reminded her of that other house where she and Max had been happy.

That is, until Max's death.

He had committed suicide after the discovery of Eustace Quinn's body in one of the outhouses at Althorpe. Quinn, an art dealer who had been planning to mount a retrospective exhibition of Gifford's work at his London gallery, had been asking too many questions about Max's past, including his relationship with Lilith, a model who had sat for him before the war.

During the investigation, Finch had discovered that, years after Lilith had returned to her husband, Max Gifford had tried to find her again. Although in the meantime she had died shortly after Danny's birth, Max had met and fallen in love with her daughter, Nina, then a seventeen-year-old schoolgirl. Believing quite wrongly, as it turned out, that Nina was his daughter and afraid that, if she found out, she would leave him, Max had murdered Quinn.

When Finch went to arrest him, he had found Max's body in the summerhouse where he had shot himself.

Soon after that, Nina had sold the house in Althorpe and bought this flat which she shared with Danny.

But she had not been able to cut herself off entirely from the

144

past. The memory of Max had continued to haunt her as the memory of Lilith had haunted Max, a ghost from his past which had been realized in paint and canvas in the portrait which had once dominated the sitting-room as it had dominated Max's bedroom at Althorpe.

Finch was glad it was gone. For him it was a painful reminder of the role he had played in Max's death, part of his own past which he had never quite managed to exorcize.

It had been replaced by another of Max's portraits, one of Nina this time, which must have been painted soon after she ran away from home to join him in London. She looked so incredibly young and innocent, seated by an open window wearing only a petticoat, the light falling pearly on her bare shoulders, her hair loose, a mass of fiery colour.

But the shadow of that other picture remained as a darker patch on the wall which extended beyond the edge of its smaller replacement like a ghost of itself.

At that moment, the door opened and Nina stood framed in its entrance; much older; her hair no longer that rich, spectacular auburn but a darker red as if it, too, had been overshadowed by that earlier image.

She wore it bundled back, not loose, tied at the nape with a bit of ribbon which didn't match her blouse. The style made her face look thinner, although she had lost weight since Max's death and anxiety over Danny had left the features even more finely drawn. But, as she dumped the tray down on to the low table and began to pour coffee into the cups, it was still possible to discern the old, warm, impulsive Nina to whom he had been attracted all those years before at Althorpe.

Finch said defensively, taking the coffee-cup from her, 'I tried to phone you a couple of times today but there was no answer.'

'Did you? When?'

'At half past seven this morning and again at about twelve o'clock.'

'Oh, Jack!' Nina looked stricken. 'I went down to the hall first thing to see if there was a letter from Danny. And I rushed out just before lunch to get some food in, just in case he turned up. What with the police arriving, I hadn't done any shopping and there was nothing to eat in the place. I'm so sorry. I was in all the rest of the day.'

It was just his luck that he'd tried to ring her on the only two occasions she'd been out of the flat, Finch thought. Sod's law at work again.

He said, 'Tell me about the police. When did they come?'

'The day before yesterday, in the afternoon. There were two of them – plain-clothes – an inspector and a sergeant from the West Midlands Drug Squad. They wanted to know about Danny – where he was living in Birmingham; how often he came down here; did he ever leave any luggage, like a suitcase or an overnight bag. I didn't know what they were on about to begin with until one of them, the inspector, asked if Danny was on drugs. I said no; not as far as I knew, which was true. I mean, I know he can do stupid things and he likes a drink, more than's good for him sometimes, but I can't believe he'd be that daft.'

'What's Danny doing with himself these days?' Finch asked, trying to sound casual.

He had not seen Nina's younger brother for years, having only met him during the Althorpe investigation but that short acquaintance had been enough to convince him that Danny was a born loser, content to drift through life sponging off other people, usually women who, for some inexplicable reason, seemed to find his inability to cope with life endearing and who took him in as they might a stray dog off the streets.

The prisons were full of people like Danny.

He and Nina rarely discussed her brother. His own professional status and his private belief that Nina would be well shot of him, combined with Nina's fierce loyalty towards Danny, inhibited both of them and an unspoken taboo had developed between them: Danny was not to be talked about.

Looking down into her coffee-cup, Nina said, 'He's got these friends in Birmingham he works for. They run some kind of second-hand car dealer's that sells fleet vehicles; you know, the cars businesses loan out to their employees. Anyway, it's Danny's job to travel round and pick the cars up

146

from various places when the firms want to trade them in. That's all I know. Danny doesn't tell me much. If there's a car to collect in the London area, he rings up and says he'll be down on Monday or whenever from Birmingham.'

'By train?'

'I suppose so. He usually arrives in the evening, stays overnight and leaves the next morning for wherever it is he has to collect the car from. The last time it was Acton.'

'When was this?'

'Three weeks ago.'

'And you say the police wanted to know if he'd ever left any luggage here?'

'That's right, but he never does. All he ever brings is an overnight bag with his shaving kit in it. He's still got his bedroom and he keeps some of his clothes here, pyjamas and shirts, stuff like that. He leaves his dirty things the next day for me to take to the launderette so they're clean for the next time he comes. I explained all that to the police. I don't know why they asked about luggage.'

Finch could make a damned good guess, though. If they suspected Danny of drug running, his account of picking up second-hand cars made a plausible cover story. Nina's flat could also have served as a useful base where the stuff might be stored. But, listening to her account, it seemed that Danny had had enough sense, or brotherly regard, not to use his sister's place for that purpose. Or perhaps he didn't need to, merely finding it a convenient place to spend the night, with free board and lodging, not to mention laundry service thrown in.

As for the story of his coming down by train, Finch suspected this was almost certainly a lie. He'd drive down from Birmingham, park the car somewhere out of sight of Nina's flat and pick it up the following morning to set off for whatever address he'd been given where the drugs were waiting to be collected.

He said, 'Did Danny tell you his address in Birmingham?'

'Only a phone number. I gave that to the police. But whenever I've tried ringing it, he's never there. A woman did answer once but she wasn't much help. She just said Danny was out and she didn't know when he'd be back. Then she rang off.'

'Did you ask Danny who she was?'

Nina looked embarrassed. 'I didn't like to. He gets angry if I ask him too many questions. He says it's none of my business. But oh, Jack, I'm so worried about him! I know he's done stupid things in the past but he's never been mixed up with anything really serious. He gets in with the wrong crowd, that's his trouble, and then he's too easily led. It's all a bit of a game to him, being on the fiddle, like going scrumping when we were children. Lots of kids are like that but they grow out of it. Danny never did. He's not really bad; he just likes a bit of excitement.'

And the easy money, Finch added silently.

As a professional policeman, he could see the inevitability of Danny's criminal career, from a whole series of shady jobs involving second-hand cars and unlicensed drinking premises to minor fraud. That sooner or later he'd finish up as part of a drug ring was hardly surprising.

Out loud, he said, 'Look, Nina, you've got to decide what you'll do if he turns up here.'

'I've thought about that,' Nina said quickly. 'I've hardly thought of anything else since the police came here. And I honestly don't know, Jack! Should I let him stay? Or should I hand him over? He'd go to prison, wouldn't he, if he was found guilty? He wouldn't get probation. And in a lot of ways, he'd deserve it. You read such terrible stories about youngsters getting hooked on drugs and having to steal or go on the streets to pay the pushers. But prison would finish him! He wouldn't be able to cope. I don't know that I can do that to him.'

Finch wasn't sure he agreed with her. He'd known a great many petty criminals like Danny who had managed to survive a term in prison, emerging at the end better qualified professionally than when they'd gone in. He doubted, too, if Nina's brother would ever reform. He was too far down that particular road to turn back.

148

'You know what my advice would be, Nina,' he said. 'But it's not up to me. You have to make up your own mind.'

She looked disappointed and he felt he'd failed her although he couldn't think what else he could have said to her under the circumstances.

'Yes, I know,' she replied.

Finch got up from his chair.

'Phone me,' he told her. 'If I'm not in, leave a message and I'll ring you back as soon as I can. I'm on an investigation at the moment so it may not be easy.'

'I'm sorry, Jack. I wouldn't have bothered you if I'd known.'

'It doesn't matter,' he said and, for the moment, he meant it. The Hampden case seemed very far away.

She went with him into the hall where, on a sudden impulse, she put her arms round his neck. They stood like this for several moments, Nina's head on his shoulder, the weight of her body pressed against his.

Surprised and moved, Finch ran his hands down her back in a consoling movement, feeling the tension in her spine, at the same time aware of his own inadequacy in dealing with her unhappiness.

As if aware of it herself, she broke away, smiling and sniffing back tears.

'Thanks for coming,' she said.

He could think of nothing to say except to repeat the words, 'Phone me.'

'Yes, I'll do that,' she assured him.

He wanted to add something more; God knows what but some remark which would have expressed his concern for her as well as his gratitude for those few seconds of intimacy when she had stood with her arms round him.

But he had left it too late. No sooner had he stepped out on to the landing than Nina closed the door and there was nothing he could do except walk away down the stairs.

At about the same time that Finch was leaving Nina's, Roz got into her car and drove to Noel's flat in West Hampstead.

149

She had tried ringing his number several times that evening but there had been no reply.

He could, of course, have gone out but Roz suspected that he was refusing to answer the phone. When things went wrong in his life, he tended to go to ground, remaining incommunicado for days at a time.

And on this occasion, it was more than a mere fit of the sulks over some girl friend who had let him down.

For her part, Roz felt that she had failed Noel totally and God knows he had needed her support more than he had ever done in the past. Hampden's murder, Annabel's betrayal, the uncertainty of his own future at Hampden and Brownlow's had affected him badly but Roz had felt incapable of supplying the sort of sympathy which she knew Noel was seeking.

The drive back from Cressetts had been a miserable experience. Noel, still in shock, had alternated between being totally silent and over-talkative, at first going on and on, about Annabel, then Hampden, punctuating the monologue with sudden questions to which she hadn't known the answers. Did she really think the police suspected him of murdering Oliver? If so, what should he do about it? And what about Annabel? And his job? Should he phone her? Should he start looking in the *Guardian* for another post? Or would it be better to wait?

To most of his questions, Roz had been forced to say she didn't know. It was up to him to decide.

She herself had felt exhausted, not only by all that had happened at Cressetts but by Noel's stress, almost panic, which was affecting his driving, adding to her own inability to cope with him. As they tore along the country roads or roared down the fast lane of the M25, she had found it impossible to concentrate on what he was saying or what her answers ought to be.

Once they reached the outskirts of London Noel had stopped talking altogether, as if he had withdrawn from her entirely, and when he had dropped her off in Earls Court he had said goodbye in a perfunctory manner.

Standing on the pavement outside her flat, Roz had

watched him drive away, ready to wave should he look back. But he hadn't.

Since then he hadn't been in touch with her or answered the phone when she rang.

Parking outside the Edwardian villa which he shared with three other young men who worked in the City like him, Roz looked up at the front window which she knew was his room. There was a light on so he was at home, damn him.

She rang his bell twice and then, pressing it for the third time, held her finger on the buzzer.

Standing in the tiny front garden, she could hear the bell ringing and ringing upstairs. But she wasn't going to leave until he answered.

He responded at last but not in quite the way she had expected.

Upstairs, the sash window was suddenly flung open and Noel's hand appeared over the sill.

'What the hell do you want?' he demanded.

'Just to talk,' Roz said. 'Come on, Noel. Let me in.'

He considered the request for a few moments while she craned her neck to look up at him.

Then he said without any apparent animosity, 'Shove off, Roz, and leave me alone.' The next moment, his head disappeared and the window was slammed down.

A passer-by who had witnessed the exchange turned to look curiously as Roz, banging the gate shut behind her, got into her car and turned on the ignition.

She felt a mixture of emotions – surprise and anger at Noel's rejection of her, uncertainty about what she should do next.

But overwhelmingly and absurdly, there was a sense of enormous relief that Noel no longer seemed to need her.

She'd miss him, of course, quite dreadfully but, thank God, it seemed that she was free of him at last.

13

The message came the following morning in the middle of a briefing, telephoned directly to Divisional Headquarters by Christie Hampden.

Frank Clayton's body had been found in the ornamental pool at Cressetts – an apparent suicide. The local station at Widford had already been informed.

'What I don't understand,' said Finch to Boyce, 'is how Clayton managed to get into the grounds in the first place. There were two uniformed men left there on duty last night.'

They were on their way to Cressetts by car, Finch having wound up the briefing and alerted Pardoe about this second case of violent death.

'Big place,' Boyce remarked, in the men's defence. 'Plenty of cover in the way of bushes. Anyone could've easily slipped into the garden without being seen.'

Which was true, as Finch acknowledged when later they walked down the lawn towards the pool. The whole area was surrounded by shrubs and trees.

The body lay face down in the water, fully dressed in jeans and a denim jacket, and looking inert and clumsy in comparison with the statue of the naked girl which glistened in the sunshine, stretched above him as if in silent exultation at this second corpse.

Even more incongruously, a sheet of folded paper had been thrust into the gap between her thighs where it stuck out like a white penis.

Finch noticed it when he was still several yards away. It had a jaunty, defiant look about it, the equivalent of a two-fingered salute. Under the circumstances, he thought it a sick joke.

'Suicide note?' Pardoe suggested.

He had evidently only just arrived himself and was seated on the coping round the pool, his medical bag at his feet. The team of SOCOs and plain-clothes men stood about, waiting for orders.

'Well,' Pardoe continued when Finch had stood contemplating the body for several moments in silence, 'if you've seen all you want, I'd like him out.'

As McCullum and Bretherton had already taken a video and still shots of the scene, Finch nodded and stepped back, making room for two of the plain-clothes men to come forward. Lifting the body out of the water, they laid it on the sheet as Pardoe knelt down to make his examination. Water from the clothes and hair ran across the black plastic in glittering streams to soak into the grass.

'Classic case of death by drowning,' Pardoe remarked with relish over his shoulder. For once, he seemed in a good humour. 'See the froth round the nose and mouth? That's always a clear sign; means he was alive when he went into the water. No sign of any injuries as far as I can see apart from some bruises on the right arm.'

'Where?' Finch asked.

'Here.' Pardoe pointed to several small pressure marks which had darkened the skin just above the wrist.

'Fingermarks?'

'Could be,' Pardoe conceded.

'Any chance it's murder, not suicide?'

'That's your decision, laddy, not mine,' Pardoe said with a grin although he relented a little to add, 'Talk to me when I've done the PM. If there are any signs of violence on the body, I'll know as soon as he's stripped and on the slab. But I can tell you right now, he wasn't knocked unconscious before he drowned. There's no injuries to the head.'

Even after the body had been taken away, it still took the chief inspector several minutes to get going. He seemed preoccupied with the surrounding scene, the trees heavy with

153

summer foliage, the long sweep of lawn leading up to the house and finally the pool itself, its white stone coping darkened with water where Clayton's body had been lifted over the edge.

The area had been cleared of the paraphernalia of the play. The lighting stands had gone. So, too, had the gilt chairs although a compacted semicircle of grass showed where they had once stood.

As for the rest of the lawn, it looked immaculate. There were no trails that he could see which might indicate that anyone, even Clayton, had walked across it in the direction of the pool. It was too late for the dew to be still lying. The sun had dried it up long ago.

All the same, he'd go through the motions, get the dog handlers in and send some of the men to make a search.

Suicide? Or murder?

If suicide, why here? Why not at the caravan or somewhere else? And why choose drowning? Clayton had a gun. Finch had seen it himself, propped up in the corner along with the gardening tools.

He turned to the local inspector from Widford who had been first on the scene.

'Who found him?'

'A chap called Teague.'

'Any sign of a white Ford pick-up round the place?'

'Not near the house. Mind you, we haven't looked for one.'

'Right!'

Turning briskly on his heel, the chief inspector started to issue orders, sending Barney off with some of the men to make a search of the grounds, with specific orders to look for Clayton's Ford. Farley and Dobson were dispatched to examine the caravan.

It was Wylie who offered to collect the note, stripping down to his shirt and underpants before wading through the thigh-deep water to extract it from between the statue's legs with a pair of tweezers.

'Odd place to put it. Looks a bit like you-know-what,'

remarked Boyce, who could be surprisingly prudish at times. 'Why stuff it in there?'

He seemed unaware of the sexual connotation behind his use of language which, given the circumstances, was apt. Finch wondered if that was what the gesture was intended to convey – a mute invitation to get stuffed.

It fitted in with his mental image of the murderer; it had that same sardonic sense of humour.

Wylie, grinning cheerfully as if he'd enjoyed his morning's paddle, had waded back, the note flattened inside a clear plastic envelope which he handed to the chief inspector.

With Boyce at his shoulder, Finch read the message through its covering film.

It stated simply: 'I've made up my mind to kill myself. I don't want to go on living anymore. Frank Clayton.'

Boyce said, 'Seems straightforward enough, assuming it's Clayton's handwriting. The bloke decided to do himself in.'

'Yes,' said Finch although he had his reservations, not only about Clayton's choice of place and method of suicide, but also about the note itself.

If Clayton had murdered Hampden, which was the obvious conclusion to be drawn from his decision to kill himself, then why hadn't he mentioned this fact in his suicide note?

'I want to talk to Christopher Hampden,' he said abruptly and set off up the lawn towards the house.

Hampden, who was waiting for them in the hall, followed the chief inspector and the sergeant into the office.

In the event, he wasn't much help.

He had heard nothing unusual during the night. In fact, it was only when Teague had told him of finding Clayton's body in the pool that he'd realized anything was wrong.

As soon as he was informed, he'd gone down to the pool with Teague to see if the man was still alive.

No; he hadn't gripped Clayton by the wrist. He'd simply felt for a pulse in the neck. Once he'd realized Clayton was dead, he'd come back to the house to phone the police.

Which meant the dogs were unlikely to pick up any trail,

Finch thought disgustedly. With both Teague and Hampden trampling about over the site, they'd've mucked up any scent.

'I'd like to have a word with Teague,' he said. 'Where will I find him?'

'He's in his workshop. I'll show you,' Hampden said and led the way across the hall and down the passage which went past the dining-room. Here the corridor, after making the dog-leg turn by the vestibule where the downstairs cloakroom was situated, continued on towards the end of the wing which appeared to be the domestic part of the house. At this point, a door, a servants' or tradesmen's entrance, opened out into a paved area.

Originally, it would have served as a stable-yard and was enclosed on three sides by a range of outbuildings, most of them converted into garages. A silver-grey BMW and a more modest Ford Granada were standing outside on the flag-stones.

Christie pointed to one of the outhouses which faced them, a two-storeyed building which, unlike the others, had an ordinary front door, not one of the up-and-over garage entrances.

'You'll find Cliff in there,' he said. 'If you want me, I'll be with my mother. You know where her room is.'

Turning abruptly away, he re-entered the house leaving Finch and Boyce to cross the yard towards Teague's workshop.

Teague let them in, standing grudgingly to one side as they entered.

The interior was large, the brick walls, or what could be seen of them, painted white. For the most part they were hidden either behind racks of metal shelves or sheets of perforated hardboard on which tools were hanging. Below them, benches extended round the entire workshop except for the far corner where an open-tread wooden staircase led to an upper floor.

Standing on one of the benches was the lighting console which Finch had last seen by the pool. Teague was evidently in the process of dismantling it, for some of the cables had been disconnected and the dimmer switches were lying loose on the work top.

'I thought all the equipment was hired,' Finch remarked.

'Not this one. I made it myself,' Teague said shortly. He seemed keen to bring the chief inspector to the point for he added, 'I suppose you're here about Clayton. D'you want to go upstairs to talk?'

The offer surprised Finch. He hadn't thought Teague would bother with such social niceties but he nodded and Teague led the way up the stairs to a small landing and from there into the main room.

Like the workshop downstairs, it was large, functional and obsessively tidy. A plain table, of the type you could buy as a flat-pack in a DIY store, stood by the window, accompanied by one stick-back chair. A single armchair, with cushions resting on a wooden frame, had been drawn up in front of an electric fire and a portable television set. Evidently Teague entertained few visitors.

There were no books and few concessions to comfort apart from an Anglepoise lamp on a bedside table and a strip of carpet by a divan which occupied the far wall.

Otherwise, the floor was bare boards, sanded, stained and scrupulously clean.

The whole effect, the white walls and ceiling, the dark floor and the minimal furniture, suggested a monk's cell, an apt comparison since there was something ascetic about Teague himself, despite his oil-stained jeans and open-necked shirt. With his lean face and brooding expression he might have been a lay brother attached to some religious order.

Even the large poster of a Harley-Davidson motor bike taped to the wall above the bed seemed to fit in with this image. It dominated the otherwise bare room like an icon or a crucifix.

They remained standing as Teague, who had his back to the window, didn't invite them to sit down.

It was clear he wasn't going to offer the chief inspector an opening, despite his invitation to accompany him upstairs, which left Finch to start the interview from cold.

He said, 'I understand from Mr Hampden that you found Clayton's body. When was that?'

'About eight o'clock this morning,' Teague replied. He did, however, volunteer the next piece of information. 'I was going to rake over the grass where the chairs had been.'

'Must have been a bit of a shock,' Finch suggested.

'Yeah,' Teague said, laconically. 'It was.'

'So what did you do?'

'I went straight to the house and told Mr Hampden. After he'd had a look and decided Clayton was dead, Mr Hampden said he'd phone the police.'

'You knew Mr Clayton?'

'Not very well. He wasn't a mate of mine.'

'But you suggested, when we talked before, that he might know something about Oliver Hampden's murder.'

Teague wasn't having that. For the first time, he showed a reaction.

'I didn't say that!' he protested. 'I just said you ought to have a talk with him; that's all.'

'About the quarrel he'd had with Oliver Hampden?'

Teague seemed embarrassed. Stuffing his hands into his pockets, he half-turned away, one shoulder lifted defensively.

'Tell me about it,' Finch said.

So far all he'd learned from Christopher Hampden and Clayton himself was the fact that two years before Clayton had worked at Cressetts as a gardener until Oliver Hampden had sacked him.

With his face still averted, Teague said, 'Clayton was in debt over some equipment he'd bought and behind with his mortgage repayments. He asked Oliver – Mr Hampden – for a loan but Mr Hampden turned him down. Clayton got angry about it and that's when Mr Hampden cancelled his contract. Anyway, the business went bust and Clayton lost the house that went with it. That's when he moved into that caravan. It was soon after that his wife left him; cleared off and took the kid with her.'

It was said abruptly as if Teague took no pleasure in passing on the story which reflected badly, Finch realized, on Oliver Hampden.

It was probably for this reason that Lady Kelling and Christopher Hampden had brushed the whole affair aside.

As for Clayton, Finch could understand his reticence over the quarrel. It gave him a good motive for murdering Oliver Hampden, a point he put to Teague.

'Did Clayton say anything to you about wanting to kill Oliver Hampden?'

'No; not to me.'

'Did he ever threaten to commit suicide?'

'No; but, like I said, he wasn't a mate of mine.'

'Any idea where he might have got into the grounds?'

'Could've been anywhere,' Teague said with a shrug. 'In places, there isn't even a fence, just bushes. He'd worked here so he knew the garden.'

It was a point which hadn't occurred to Finch and one which he pressed further. 'You said you've worked here yourself for six or seven years so you'd've been here at the same time as Clayton was under contract as a gardener?'

The question seemed to have no significance for Teague who answered in the same offhand manner, 'Yeah; that's right.'

His attitude baffled Finch. Even though he had worked with Clayton, he seemed untouched by the man's death and his own discovery of the body, almost as if Clayton had been a stranger to him. And yet most people would have been affected. In Teague's case, there was nothing; not even, as far as Finch could judge, any feeling of animosity towards the man.

As Teague had expressed it, Clayton wasn't a mate and, as far as he was concerned, that was that.

The chief inspector was casting about in his mind how to get round this deadlock when he heard the door downstairs open and Kyle's voice call out, 'Are you there, sir?'

Going on to the landing, Finch looked down the stairs to see Kyle standing just inside the workshop.

'Sorry to interrupt you, sir. Mr Hampden said you'd be here. There's something I think you ought to see.'

159

When the chief inspector and Boyce had joined him outside in the yard out of Teague's hearing, Kyle added, 'It's Clayton's pick-up. At least, we think it's his. We found it in a lane on the far side of the grounds.'

They went on foot, Kyle leading the way across the lawn and through the shrubbery at the far side where they climbed over a low fence into a narrow lane which sloped gently uphill, following the lie of the land.

The lane looked little used and, as far as Finch could see, led nowhere much except to a farm. Clayton's van had been drawn up on the grass verge about fifty yards along it, close to a stile on the far side of which a footpath led up a wooded slope towards the top of the incline.

Finch and Boyce prowled round the Ford. The doors were locked and there was no sign of any disturbance either inside the cab or in the surrounding area. No struggle appeared to have taken place. It would seem that Clayton had merely parked the pick-up, and badly too – he had run the front of it into a tangle of brambles – before presumably making off on foot for Cressetts.

By the path? As Clayton had chosen to leave the Ford near it, it seemed likely.

Clambering over the stile, Finch set off along it, Boyce and Kyle at his heels, following its route through the trees to the top of the hill where it emerged from the wood into open meadowland. Here the chief inspector halted.

From that point he had a view down the slope towards Cressetts. The back of the house was visible, including part of the terrace and the lawn which led down to the pool. But not the pool itself. That was hidden behind the trees which formed the boundary to that part of the garden.

Moving on a few yards, he stopped again.

This time, with the angle of vision slightly changed, he could now see a wider stretch of the garden. The vista had opened up to encompass the whole of the terrace and, to the right, the circular pool, the sunlight flashing on the water as if to signal its presence.

It was Boyce who found the hide. He had wandered a few

yards off the path towards a clump of low bushes to find his own vantage point – to Finch's exasperation as the sergeant's bulky figure was blocking his view.

He was about to call out to him to shift himself when Boyce forestalled him.

'Come and look at this!' he shouted. There was an urgency and an excitement in his voice.

Finch and Kyle set off down the slope towards him.

He was standing a few feet from the bushes, pointing at the ground where the grass was flattened into an elongated shape as if someone had been lying there. Stubbed into the turf nearby were seven or eight cigarette butts.

Finch squatted down over them. They looked old, stained by damp, the paper brittle where it had later dried out in the sun. Some were mere empty tubes, the threads of tobacco having spilt out. And they were quite obviously handrolled.

There was no doubt in Finch's mind that they were Clayton's although DNA tests would prove it.

But what the hell had Clayton been doing, lying up here behind the bushes?

Still squatting, Finch bent his head, craning it sideways so that he was looking along the same line of vision as Clayton would have had. It was then that he saw the cleaner wood where some of the twigs had been snapped off to form a roughly circular hole at the base of the bush.

Awkwardly he got to his feet, one hand on the small of his back where the muscles were jumping.

'It's a sniper's nest,' he said.

Boyce was inclined to scoff. 'Come off it!'

'I tell you it bloody is. Anyone lying here would have a clear view down the slope to the back of the house. And don't forget Clayton owned a ·223 Ruger and that's a powerful weapon. I want McCullum and Bretherton over here to video the scene and take stills. And we'll get the SOCOs in to make a search. Kyle, you stay here; make sure no one comes trampling about over the place.'

On their return to Cressetts, Finch stayed long enough to confer with the SOCOs and to dispatch a couple of the plain-clothes men to search Clayton's caravan for the gun before, leaving Boyce in charge, he drove back to Chelmsford alone to attend the post-mortem on Clayton.

Suicide or murder?

The question still ran through his mind.

It was to remain unanswered.

The discovery of the sniper's nest had delayed the chief inspector and by the time he arrived, to his relief the PM was over and Pardoe was cleaning up in the sluice room.

'I still can't help you there,' Pardoe told him, vigorously swilling his hands and arms. 'All I can tell you is it's definitely a case of drowning. The lungs were full of water. And there were no signs of violence on the body apart from those bruises just above the right wrist. How they got there is your business but I'd guess he'd been grasped fairly tightly by the arm, not long before he died either. I'll give you this for nothing, though – the alcohol content of the stomach was high; whisky by the smell of it. He must have been very drunk when he went into the water; practically blotto, if you want my opinion. Time of death? Anywhere between ten o'clock last night and three o'clock this morning.'

Finch thanked him and left.

There was no point in returning to Cressetts. By the time he arrived there, Boyce and the others would probably have finished and would be ready to leave.

Instead, he drove back to Divisional Headquarters where he shut himself up in his office, relieved to be alone for once to review the case in his own time with no one else, not even Boyce, to interrupt his train of thought.

Clayton's death was so damned iffy anyway that he doubted if he could have expressed his ideas out loud without having the opportunity to think them through first.

On the face of it, the case seemed straightforward.

He now had a motive. Teague had given him that and it hung together. As a result of what had happened between him and Hampden, Clayton had set up the sniper's nest on the hill overlooking Cressetts with the intention of murdering

162

his ex-employer by picking him off with the rifle as he sat on the terrace or walked about the garden.

But he hadn't done so.

Why?

There were several possible reasons, all of which were plausible. The right opportunity might not have presented itself. After all, Hampden only came down to the house at weekends and even then not on a regular basis. When he was in residence, he might not have appeared in the garden at a time that Clayton was lying in wait for him.

Then there was the question of the range. He'd have to check with a firearms expert, of course, but Finch had his doubts that even a ·223 Ruger could have picked off a target at that distance. It must have been over 200 yards from the sniper's nest to the garden. It would have had to be a lucky shot to kill Hampden.

Perhaps Clayton was aware of this himself, which was why he'd accepted the part in the play when Noel Fielding had offered it to him, abandoning the idea of shooting Hampden and deciding instead to murder him during the performance. He'd've been given a copy of the play so he'd've known that, while the second act was being played in the garden, there'd be an interval of nearly half an hour while Hampden was alone in the dining-room before the third act began.

That line of reasoning opened up the probability that Clayton was lying when he'd said he'd seen Hampden alive shortly before the prop gun was fired and the garden scene ended.

Taking that as fact, the rest of the theory followed a logical sequence. Having established the first part of his alibi by remaining in the hall talking to Wyvern, Clayton had then gone to the dining-room, presumably entering through the door at the back of the room, with the intention of murdering Hampden.

It was at this point in the theory that the first problem arose.

What had Clayton done next?

He must have walked the length of the room, mounted the

stage and, taking the curtain cord from its hook, stepped behind Hampden's chair and strangled him.

And what about Hampden? What had he been doing while all this was going on?

According to Pardoe, he'd been murdered while he was sitting down and that fact didn't square up with what he himself had found out from Teague.

Hampden and Clayton had quarrelled; as a consequence, Hampden had cancelled Clayton's contract.

Given those circumstances, would Hampden have remained seated while Clayton approached him?

Finch wasn't sure about that. It seemed out of keeping with the rest of the scenario.

But in the face of the other evidence, there was nothing he could do except leave that part of the theory on one side while he moved on to what must have happened afterwards.

Once Hampden was dead, it would have taken Clayton only a few seconds to slip back through the hall to the front door where Roz Bennet had seen him standing on the steps and smoking a cigarette, when she came out of the office.

That way, he'd established the second part of his alibi which he had backed up by the lie that he'd seen Hampden alive shortly before.

So far, so good. With the one reservation, that part of the theory hung together fairly satisfactorily.

It was when he turned to Clayton's own death that he came up against more major flaws and his sense of uneasiness increased.

Having murdered Hampden, Clayton then decided to commit suicide; not on the face of it improbable. He had, after all, lost his business as well as his wife and child and it may have been his intention from the time he set up the sniper's nest to kill himself soon after Hampden's death.

It was the manner of the suicide which Finch still couldn't come to terms with.

All right – he was prepared to accept the idea that Clayton might have chosen to kill himself at Cressetts to bring home the fact that it was Hampden who had caused his bankruptcy and the breakdown of his marriage: a last gesture of defiance.

But why drowning? Why not the gun?

Or had he been so drunk that he hadn't dared use it in case he bungled his own death?

Possible.

There was still, however, the suicide note to take into account. There was no reference in that to Hampden's murder.

Shouldn't there have been?

If I were in Clayton's shoes, Finch thought, I'd've made it damned clear to whoever found my body that I'd murdered Hampden and why I'd done it.

And then there were the bruises on the right arm, just above the wrist. They didn't fit in with the suicide theory either. Someone had gripped Clayton's arm – and tightly, too; in Finch's book, that suggested murder.

But were those fingermarks enough evidence to hang a whole case on?

It was one of the aspects of the investigation which he'd have to discuss with Boyce on his return.

Now that he'd got his thoughts in better order, Finch turned his attention to a large manilla envelope lying on his desk which contained the first contact prints of the still photographs McCullum had taken at the various scenes.

Tipping them out, he shuffled through them. They were mostly of the dining-room, long shots of the stage as well as close-ups of Hampden's body, but they also included prints of the other photographs which McCullum had taken by the pool.

He flipped through these last prints quickly, intending to return and examine more carefully those taken at the actual scene of the murder.

God knows why one of them should have caught his attention. In view of Clayton's death, it shouldn't have been relevant to the inquiry and yet he found himself staring down at it; or rather at one small portion which, because of the angle of the camera, stood out quite clearly in the close-up.

It took a moment or two for its significance to dawn on him.

Then he said out loud in a voice full of surprised exultation, even though it knocked his carefully constructed theory to kingdom come, 'So that was how it was done!' before adding with a grudging admiration, 'The cheeky sod!'

14

Boyce said, 'Are you sure?'

They were in the car, driving back to Cressetts from where the sergeant had only just returned. He had barely set foot inside the office when Finch had bundled him out again.

'I mean,' he went on, 'there's not much to go on, is there? If you want my opinion, my money's still on Clayton as Hampden's murderer. Incidentally, we didn't find the gun. It wasn't in the caravan or the Ford. So that's missing for a start. And what about the suicide note? Where does that fit in?'

He sounded aggrieved as if Finch had deliberately set out to prove him wrong.

'I don't know, Tom,' Finch admitted. He was still having trouble himself with the note. 'We'll have to ask when we get there, won't we? It must fit in somewhere. The rest of it hangs together.'

In the half-hour he'd had to wait for the sergeant to return, he'd gone over his theory as critically as Boyce himself was now doing, testing it out by playing his own devil's advocate. Even so, most of it made sense.

There was the question of why Hampden had been sitting down behind the desk when he had been murdered. That was now answered. And another – how the murderer had known Annabel Thorpe wasn't waiting on the terrace to make her entrance as she should have been but had nipped off out of sight round the corner of the house to the cloakroom.

It explained, too, the bruises on Clayton's arm although he

167

still wasn't quite sure why the suicide note had been placed between the statue's thighs.

He'd had trouble as well with the motive and, as if Boyce had tuned into his thoughts, the sergeant chose that moment to ask, 'And what about motive? I can't see there is one.'

Finch said, playing it down, 'We'll sort that out when we get there. I tell you, Tom, the whole thing's feasible. I checked with Willis.'

'Willis? The duty sergeant? What the hell does he know about it?'

'Don't you remember? Last Christmas he was selling tickets for that pantomime in aid of the Spastics Society. He helped to organize the production.' They had arrived at Cressetts and Finch broke off to add, 'Don't use the main entrance. Go in the back way.'

The drive forked at the courtyard gates, a branch of it leading round to the back of the house where it swung sharply left into the stable-yard and where they parked and got out.

There was no sign of Teague. The door to his workshop was locked and when Finch peered through the window, cupping his hands to see past the glass, the place looked empty.

'He's gone,' a voice said behind them.

It was Christopher Hampden who had appeared at the kitchen entrance and was on the point of walking towards them.

'Any idea where?' Finch asked casually. 'There's a couple of questions I wanted to ask him.'

'I don't know,' Christie replied. 'He cleared off about half an hour ago. You'd better come into the house. As a matter of fact, I've been trying to get in touch with you but they told me you'd already left. Then I heard your car.'

As he led the way down the passage, he added over his shoulder, 'What put you on to him?'

I might ask the same of you, Finch thought.

There was no time to reply. Hampden had opened the door to his mother's sitting-room and was ushering them inside.

Lady Kelling was sitting in the same chair by the window in the same straight-backed pose. She might not have moved since the last time Finch had spoken to her the day before. Her face looked more hollow as if in the intervening hours some of the flesh had been scooped away. But her style hadn't changed.

'Sit down,' she told them and as the three of them obeyed like schoolboys summoned to an interview with a formidable parent, she turned to address Finch. 'How much do you know, Chief Inspector?'

It was time to come clean; and also time to take control of the interview.

'I know Teague murdered your son,' Finch replied. 'I know, too, how he managed to arrange it. I also know that he murdered Clayton. For the moment, though, I'm not sure why he killed them. What I need from you, Lady Kelling, is the answer to that question and a few more. But what I must find out first of all, either from you or Mr Hampden, is where Teague is. I have to find him.'

It was Christopher Hampden who answered. 'I told you, he left about half an hour ago.'

'How? On foot?'

'By car. His car.'

'Type? Colour?'

'A dark blue Granada.'

'Registration number?'

To Finch's surprise, it was Lady Kelling who supplied this last piece of information. Almost before he had finished writing down the final number, Boyce was on his feet, notebook in hand, making for the door.

Finch remained seated. There was no need for the two of them to put out a general alert to all patrol cars, especially those in the Widford area, to keep a look-out for Teague's vehicle.

There was a moment's silence after the sergeant left the room in which Finch felt strangely relaxed. There was nothing more he could do. The search was someone else's responsibility and he could sit back and let the interview take its course, with a little guidance now and then.

As he had expected, Lady Kelling spoke first.

169

She said, 'You asked about Clifford's motives, Chief Inspector, but before you can understand those, you have to appreciate what my elder son was like. Although I loved him, that didn't stop me from knowing what Oliver was or what effect he had on other people. He was like my father in many respects – the same hunger to succeed, the same charm which he used to control and manipulate others and the same ruthlessness towards anyone who failed. They both hated failure. Perhaps it reminded them too much of their own need for success and what might happen to them if they didn't achieve it.

'In my father's case, it was understandable. He was a self-made man who'd worked his way up from relatively humble beginnings to become one of the most popular and highest-paid writers before the war. He travelled abroad; he bought this house where he entertained the rich and influential. But at a price. Along the way, those who were no longer any use to him were discarded – former friends, women he'd slept with; even my mother.

'He was a great womanizer. He had charm, you see, and this need to keep proving to himself that he was successful. It killed my mother. It's no longer fashionable to believe people can die of a broken heart. But they can be killed little by little through neglect and the wearing away of any sense of self-worth. My mother's death was attributed to cancer but that was only the physical symptom of a very deep unhappiness.'

She turned to her younger son who was sitting with his elbows on his knees, silently staring down at the carpet. 'You weren't aware of any of this, were you, Christie? All you and Oliver remembered were the good times you'd had here – the pony rides and the Christmas parties. That's why I didn't want Oliver to put on the festival in memory of his grandfather. My own memories of him were too painful; not the charades and the games but my mother dying slowly upstairs while some other woman shared your grandfather's bed.'

'Then why did you bring us here to live after my father died?' Christie asked. It was almost an accusation.

'Because I had no choice until I remarried. You won't remember this either but he left only debts. Your grandfather offered to settle them and to pay Oliver's and your school fees if I'd agree to live at Cressetts. He wanted someone to act as his hostess and give him respectability. That way, he could still bring his women here without causing a scandal. It was a form of blackmail, of course. And perhaps you're right; I should have resisted.'

At this point, Boyce returned, giving the chief inspector a small nod to indicate that Divisional Headquarters had been informed. As he sat down, Finch took the opportunity to ask a question.

'Is this why you thought your son wouldn't marry Miss Thorpe?'

'Of course, Chief Inspector. Oliver had had a great many affairs, usually with married women, his way of avoiding any real commitment. But he was looking for a wife. Like his grandfather, he needed respectability. In Oliver's case, there was another reason. He was also hoping for some recognition for his business activities – an OBE, perhaps later even a knighthood. He'd made all the right moves – contributed to party funds, persuaded his fellow directors to subsidize one or two arts ventures. The G. B. Russell Festival was part of the scheme. I believe the expression is "putting your name about". All he lacked was a wife with the right social and financial background. Annabel Thorpe was his first try-out.'

'Try-out?' Finch asked. The phrase sounded oddly contemporary coming from Lady Kelling.

'That's what it amounted to. She was the daughter of Bernard Thorpe, the financier. Oliver brought her down here to see how she fitted in against the background of Cressetts but I'm afraid she didn't quite suit. Although Oliver was probably unaware of it himself, what he was really looking for was someone like my mother, a much more pliant woman who would tolerate his infidelities without complaining or running to a lawyer. Annabel was much too independent. Had they married, she would almost certainly have divorced him, causing the sort of scandal he was anxious to avoid. I realized that.

171

So, too, in his way, did Oliver. She would have been dropped eventually and some other woman put through her paces.'

'But not Mary Hogarth?'

'Oh, no, Chief Inspector. Mary was nowhere in the running. She'd been useful to Oliver in the past but there was no thought of marriage on Oliver's part. She, too, would have been dropped, together with Noel Fielding, once the festival was over and Oliver had no further need of them. And there had been no affair with Mary. There was no need for that.'

Christie gave a wry little smile as if he understood the implications of his mother's remark although Finch failed to pick them up.

'I don't understand,' he said.

'It's not necessary to sleep with a woman in order to keep her loyalty and Oliver was very skilful at winning people over until, that is, he had no further use for them. It didn't take much in Mary's case – a smile, an air of intimacy. You see, Oliver was very adept at finding people who were desperate to be loved or needed. He could pick them out at first glance. But both Mary and Noel Fielding made the mistake of being failures, Mary because she wasn't pretty enough, Fielding because he wasn't the high-flyer he should have been. Clayton was another failure.'

'Ah, yes; Clayton,' Finch said pointedly.

The emphasis wasn't lost on Lady Kelling who for a moment looked uncharacteristically flustered. 'We should have told you about him from the beginning. I realize that and apologize. It wasn't a deliberate attempt to deceive you or withhold information. We wanted – well, I'm not sure if either Christie or I ever rationalized it and it certainly wasn't discussed between us – to protect both Clayton and Oliver. Clayton had suffered enough at Oliver's hands. As for Oliver, I suppose we wanted to protect him as well; or, at least, his memory. You know the story?'

'I heard it from Teague.'

'Yes,' Lady Kelling said as if she perfectly understood. 'It was such a ridiculously small sum Clayton wanted to borrow – three thousand pounds. Oliver could easily have afforded it.

But to him, it was nothing more than a business deal. He talked to Clayton; went over the books with him before deciding that he was undercapitalized and the business wasn't worth saving. Of course, he didn't know then that Clayton's wife would leave him and take the child with her. But the whole episode was deeply humiliating for Clayton, having to go cap in hand to Oliver. He was always independent even when he worked here; another quality which didn't exactly endear him to Oliver. He took the refusal badly and said things which he may have regretted afterwards. Oliver used the excuse that his work wasn't satisfactory to cancel his contract. But neither Christie nor I believed he'd murdered Oliver.'

'No?' said Finch. 'Why was that?'

It seemed to him a hell of an assumption for them to make and he was tempted to tell them as much. Not that it would do any good. He'd only antagonize them – Lady Kelling in particular – and he needed their co-operation. For the same reason, he decided to keep quiet about the sniper's nest Clayton had set up on the hill overlooking the garden. He'd drop that particular bombshell into their safe little world later.

Lady Kelling was saying, 'Oliver was sitting down when he was murdered. If Clayton had come anywhere near him, Oliver would have got to his feet and confronted him. I knew my son, Chief Inspector. He was a tall man and he always used his height if ever he found himself in a face-to-face situation. Whoever killed him had to be someone he trusted.'

'And someone who had good reason to come on to the stage at that particular moment in the play,' Finch added.

There was no need for him to explain that Hampden had been expecting Teague to enter through the terrace doors to take over the light and sound effects for the last act.

He had come to this conclusion himself although he wasn't surprised that Lady Kelling had followed the same line of reasoning. Right from the beginning, he had realized that she was nobody's fool.

Sitting there by the window in her black dress, she must have gone over the evidence in very much the same way as he

173

had done, examining each suspect in turn before dismissing them. Of course, in her case, she had an advantage over him. She'd known the victim intimately. And she was also in the position of being closely acquainted with the murderer.

He said, 'What made you think it was Teague?'

It was too blunt an approach. Finch saw her frown slightly as if in disapproval before she answered.

'I spoke before of Oliver's skill at making use of people and ensuring their loyalty while it suited him. Clifford Teague was one of them. Since he's worked here, I've learnt a little about his background. He was from a deprived family – an inadequate mother and a father who drank heavily. For a time he and his brothers were taken into care. When Oliver met him and offered him the job of handyman, he was working in a garage in Widford. Right from the start, I think Oliver realized Clifford was a deeply unhappy man with an enormous grudge against life who'd be grateful for whatever Oliver did to help him. The relationship was wrong from the beginning.

'Over the years, they built up what I can only describe as a conspiracy between them. I saw it happening but there was nothing I could do to stop it. It was too subtle and there was so little on the surface to object to. It was one of the reasons I stayed on here. I knew that once Oliver married and no longer needed me, I'd be discarded like everybody else. Oh, don't misunderstand me, Chief Inspector. It would have been done with the greatest tact and entirely for my own good. I should have been consulted over which I preferred – a house in the village or a flat in London. There were times when I was tempted to take the matter into my own hands and leave on my own terms. It was only because Clifford was here that I decided to stay. Oliver's relationship with him made me deeply uneasy.'

'Why?' Finch asked. He had an inkling of the truth but it was largely guesswork. He needed her confirmation.

She said, 'I think Clifford is what is known as a latent homosexual. No doubt a psychologist could tell you the exact term. Clifford himself was unaware of it. His own background and upbringing had made him repress that side of his nature.

But Oliver knew; perhaps only subconsciously although I can't be sure that he wasn't fully aware of what he was doing. I have few illusions about my elder son. I'd seen my own father manipulate others too often not to recognize the same trait in Oliver. Games, Chief Inspector. It all comes down to the games people like him and my father played with other people.'

Or with themselves, Finch thought, remembering Nina's remarks about Danny. 'And in Teague's case?' he asked out loud.

'Oh, in his case the game was complex and subtle, as I've said. Teague had a contempt for women; part of his repressed homosexuality, I imagine. Oliver encouraged it – out of amusement, perhaps, but I think, deep down, he shared Clifford's dislike of them.'

'Out of fear of being dominated?' Finch suggested.

Lady Kelling looked at him sharply with a surprised expression as if acknowledging for the first time that this stocky figure sitting opposite her with his undistinguished features was worthy of her admiration.

'You are probably right,' she admitted, 'and I may be to blame for Oliver's attitude.'

'Tell me about the games,' Finch said. This was not the occasion to analyse Lady Kelling's relationship with her elder son any more than it had been his business to lay the responsibility for Danny's behaviour on Nina's shoulders.

She seemed relieved that he had turned the conversation away from herself.

'Like a lot of men, he liked to run women down, making amused little comments about their incompetence but turning it into a joke so that it was difficult to object without appearing over-sensitive oneself. Mary Hogarth in particular came in for such remarks – her inability to park a car properly, for example. They were always said in Clifford's presence and the two of them would laugh. I used to hear them sometimes and I disliked it. There was an unpleasant sound about it as if, as I'd said, there was a conspiracy between them. Apart from the disloyalty to Mary, I felt Oliver was leading Clifford on.

175

'Then there was the strange way Oliver would defer to Clifford about anything to do with cars or machinery – the things Clifford was good at. And he'd praise him in front of others. "Cliff's done a wonderful job with that." Can you see what Oliver was doing? He was manoeuvring Clifford into an impossible role, almost like that of the dominant male in a homosexual relationship, as if it were he, not Clifford, who was dependent. Don't ask me why he did it. Perhaps it amused him. Oliver liked to have control over other people and, by acting as he did, he had Clifford in his power as much as he had Mary Hogarth and the others.'

Listening to her, Finch had his own theory about Oliver Hampden's behaviour although he had no intention of expressing it. To his ears, it sounded as if there were masochistic elements in Hampden's relationship with Teague, a similar urge which sent otherwise respectable business men to prostitutes to be whipped and humiliated.

'And then,' he said, 'your son brought Annabel Thorpe to the house and began his affair with her.'

He had been looking for a motive and there it was. There was no need for further explanation. Teague, already deeply confused over his own feelings towards Oliver Hampden, must have felt betrayed by this behaviour; fearful, too, that if Hampden married, he might lose his place at Cressetts along with that special relationship which the two of them had built up. Add to that an obsessive and brooding personality and you had the makings of a killer.

'When did you suspect him of your son's murder?' he asked.

'Not to begin with. It seemed impossible that Clifford could have done it. He was by the pool, working the light and sound effects when Oliver was murdered. He didn't have the opportunity. If I suspected anyone, it was Noel Fielding. Oliver had gone out of his way to humiliate him over Annabel Thorpe. It was only after Frank Clayton's body was found this morning that I began to think Clifford might have killed them both. That note, Chief Inspector! Only Clifford could have done something like that. It expressed all Clifford's contempt for women and their sex. And then I remembered something he always said when he was angry or upset – "I'm choked off." '

She stopped suddenly as if the words had become strangled in her own throat.

Christopher Hampden put a hand on her arm and seemed about to suggest that he escort her from the room. But she waved him away with an abrupt gesture which also indicated that he should take up the account on her behalf.

He said, 'At the time, my mother said nothing to me about her suspicions except that she thought Cliff was mad and she wanted him out of the house. That was earlier this morning, before you arrived. I rang headquarters and they told me you were on your way over here. So I went across to the workshop just to make sure Teague was still there. He was mending the motor mower when I went in. I know I shouldn't have said anything; I realize that now. I should have waited for you to arrive. But, since I was there, I had to think up some excuse for seeing him.'

'What did you say?' Finch asked sharply. He suspected that Christopher Hampden hadn't been able to resist playing his own little game, however dangerous it might have been.

'Nothing much. "Everything going all right, Cliff?" Something like that. And then I made some comment about Clayton because Cliff had found him and I thought it'd look odd if I didn't mention him. So I simply said I couldn't understand why Clayton had killed himself here. He must have had some grudge against us because of Oliver. All the time, Cliff said nothing. He just went on working at that bloody mower without looking at me. Then suddenly he seemed to explode. God, the things he said! About Clayton but mostly about Oliver; how it wasn't his fault; it was Oliver who had screwed everything up. Those were his words, Chief Inspector. "If your bloody brother hadn't screwed everything up, nothing would have happened." He'd got a spanner in his hand and I thought he was going to use it on me. As I backed off, he pushed past me, got into his car and drove off.'

'Did he say anything else?' Finch asked.

'No; a lot of it was just abuse. But there was one remark

about Clayton which I didn't follow. He said, "Clayton was watching you. You didn't know that, did you. He'd've got Oliver first if he'd had the chance."'

Finch and Boyce were on their feet simultaneously, the sergeant making straight for the door, Finch pausing long enough to say to Hampden and Lady Kelling, 'Stay in the house! Don't either of you go on to the terrace or into the garden. You understand that? Teague's armed and dangerous. Keep indoors!'

As the door slammed behind them and they ran for the yard where their car was parked, Boyce gave vent to his feelings. 'Bloody hell! You think Teague's got Clayton's gun?'

'We don't know that for sure but I'm not going to risk it,' Finch replied. He expressed some of his own anger. 'Damn Hampden! Why couldn't he have left Teague alone? If he hadn't interfered, we could have picked Teague up at the workshop; no bother. Lady Kelling's right. The man's mad; probably paranoid; anything could have set him off.'

They had reached the car and as they got in, he added, 'You drive, Tom. But park well away from that footpath up to the sniper's nest. I don't fancy a bullet through the head. On the way, I'll get on the radio to headquarters. Thanks to Hampden we're going to need back-up and an armed bloody unit.'

15

It was not surprising that the patrol cars hadn't found Teague's Ford, even if they'd driven along this minor road looking for it. He had taken it well off the lane into the wood, not far from the footpath, and had parked it behind some scrubby undergrowth where it was hidden.

Finch and Boyce parked their own car a good 200 yards away before approaching Teague's vehicle on foot. There was no sign of him, nor, when they looked in through the windows, could they see the gun lying on the seats or on the floor.

After trying the doors and finding them locked, Boyce immobilized the Granada by the simple method of letting the air out of the tyres. The two men then retreated along the grass verge to their own car as silently as they had arrived to wait for the tactical firearms unit.

The TFU arrived about twenty minutes later, accompanied by Barber, the police surgeon, and led by Harrison, a uniformed inspector.

In an impromptu roadside conference, Finch gave a brief account of the situation, describing the position of the sniper's nest and the cover offered by the nearby wood.

'And let me approach Teague first,' he added. 'I've interviewed him a couple of times, so he knows me, and I've trained as a negotiator. With a bit of luck, I think I can talk him into giving himself up. If we turn up mob-handed, God knows what he might do.'

He was less confident than he sounded.

God alone knew what Teague would do anyway. All Finch had to rely on was his own instinct that Teague would hesitate to shoot an unarmed man in cold blood; not much of a consolation when he'd already murdered twice and on the first occasion with a degree of calculation.

After a discussion, Barber and Harrison agreed, Harrison less willingly than the doctor, and the group of men set out, walking in single file up the footpath to the wood at the top of the slope.

Here Finch waited until the others had taken up their positions under cover of the trees and undergrowth before he walked forward to the edge of the copse.

As he emerged from the trees he could see Teague twenty yards ahead of him off the path in the shelter of the bushes where Boyce had discovered the sniper's nest the previous day.

As Clayton must have done before him, Teague was lying on his stomach, facing the small gap cut between the twigs, from which position he had a clear view down the slope towards the terrace and the lawn behind Cressetts. He was holding Clayton's gun loosely in his right hand but ready to bring it up against his shoulder should anyone appear below in the garden.

All his senses must have been alert, straining for the smallest sound from any direction, for even though Finch approached him from the rear, his footsteps deadened on the grass, Teague was aware of his presence. Rolling quickly over, he swung his legs round so that in no more than a couple of swift movements he was facing the chief inspector, crouched on one knee, the gun held steady and pointing straight at him.

Finch halted and held out his hands in a defensive gesture to show they were empty.

'I'm not armed, Teague,' he said, raising his voice more than was necessary in order that his words would also carry to the armed men hidden in the trees behind him, although what they would do if Teague chose to fire he had no idea. It was a small comfort to remember he was wearing a bulletproof vest.

'Bugger off!' Teague shouted.

180

'I only want to talk to you about Clayton,' Finch told him.

While he had been waiting for the TFU to arrive, he had spent the time thinking about the best way to approach Teague and had decided that Clayton's death was a less dangerous subject than Hampden's. That was too explosive. But Clayton's murder was different, a spur-of-the-moment killing and one which, or so Finch fervently hoped, Teague wouldn't regard with quite the same emotion.

The police surgeon had agreed with him. At least, he had said it was worth a try.

He called out, 'He was drunk, wasn't he? The post-mortem proved that.'

'He was a fool,' Teague replied, his voice contemptuous. 'All that crap about his wife and child! He came round last night to my place, half-pissed; went on and on about them for bloody hours; how much he loved them and how he'd thought about killing Oliver and then himself. Just frigging talk! That's all it was. Nothing but a game! He told me he'd been up here with the gun. He brought it with him, and the suicide note he'd written. He showed it to me. Then he said he'd changed his mind. He couldn't be sure of killing Oliver at that distance. D'you know what he was going to do instead to get his own back? Walk out on that last act of the play and refuse to take part. It was bloody pathetic!'

Finch stood listening, head cocked at an attentive angle, hands held loosely at his side, trying to convey just by his stance that he offered no threat, merely a sympathetic presence.

He was comforted a little by Teague's willingness to talk. Or perhaps Clayton's murder had touched off some deep chord in Teague. Clayton might not have been a mate, as Teague had said, but the two men had worked together and that could have counted for something. There was a shared bond, too, in Oliver Hampden's treatment of them both.

At the same time, Finch was thinking that Teague's last remark might account for Clayton's decision to look in on Hampden as he had waited on the stage, shortly before his murder, for the last act of the play to begin.

Was it a sudden impulse on Clayton's part to gloat silently over his former employer, knowing that shortly afterwards he intended walking out on the production?

It was a possible explanation.

But he said nothing, letting Teague run on.

Teague was saying, 'I'd got a bottle of whisky and we drank it between us, me going on about how badly Oliver'd treated me just to keep him going and thinking all the time what a bloody fool he was. And then he said, "You killed him, didn't you?" Just like that; straight out. He passed out on me after that. So I thought I'd dump him in the pool, in case he talked. That's what he'd wanted, hadn't he? To die? So I carried him down there and shoved him in.'

'And left Clayton's suicide note?' Finch asked.

'Yeah,' Teague said and laughed.

It had a chilling sound, full of that triumphant contempt which Lady Kelling had described.

Although the chief inspector waited, Teague said nothing more about Clayton's death and Finch assumed that as far as Teague was concerned, it was enough. Clayton had guessed the truth and for that reason he was too dangerous to be allowed to live. And perhaps, too, he had deserved to die because he'd been a failure in Oliver Hampden's opinion.

If that was the case, then Teague and Hampden had indeed created a conspiracy between them which had grown like some monstrous fungus to poison all their relationships, not just with each other but with everyone else they met.

The explanation also accounted for the bruises on Clayton's wrist where Teague must have grasped the unconscious man as he slung him over his shoulder.

God knows how he'd managed to evade the two uniformed men left on duty although it wouldn't have been too difficult. The gardens were large. Teague only had to wait until both men were patrolling some distant part of the grounds before, using the natural cover, he'd carried Clayton across the lawn.

'And then there was Oliver Hampden,' Finch continued, keeping his voice conversational. 'He was a fool, too, wasn't he, bringing that woman down to Cressetts, playing his own

stupid games? So he had to die. It was clever how you arranged it, building that console with those jackplug sockets on
the side of the box so you could control the lights at a distance.
Because that's how you worked it, wasn't it? That way, it
looked as if you'd got an alibi. You couldn't have murdered
Hampden. You were down at the pool when he died, working
the lighting effects.'

'Found that out, did you?'

'I saw the sockets on a close-up photo of the console,' Finch
explained simply. 'They reminded me of the outlet on my
video-recorder where the remote-control box can be plugged
in. That's what first put me on to the idea. Then I checked with
someone I know who's done a bit of amateur stage production
and he confirmed it.'

He didn't bother to add the other details which Willis had
given him – how just two dimmer switches, connected to
lengths of cable and plugged into the console, could be carried
to any distance and used to control the lights round the pool.
Teague would know all that. After all, he'd set the system up.

'I'm not sure about the sound, though,' Finch continued.
'How did you manage to fade in the music? There was no jack
socket on the tape recorder.'

'Not so frigging clever after all, are you, mister bloody
detective?' Teague sounded triumphant. 'I didn't need a re-
mote control for that. I knew how long the scene would last.
I'd timed it. It just meant re-recording the music on to a new
tape. I did that on Saturday morning before we went off to the
church. Then all I had to do when that garden scene was being
played was switch on the recorder and let it run. There was a
few minutes of silence, long enough to give that woman
Oliver was screwing around with time to walk off the set and
for Wyvern to say his last line before the music started up and
then faded out. By then, I'd already left.'

'Yes; clever that,' Finch said. It hadn't occurred to him that
the explanation could be so simple. 'There's one other thing I
don't understand. How were you sure Miss Thorpe wouldn't
wait on the terrace as she was supposed to? You couldn't have

known she'd slip round the corner to the cloakroom and leave the way clear for you to get into the dining-room.'

'I didn't; not to begin with,' Teague replied. 'When I first got the idea, I was going to go in that way myself, by the cloak-room door at the back of the house. She wouldn't have seen me crossing the garden. There's plenty of bushes. Then I'd have gone into the dining-room through the door off the passage.'

'Risky,' Finch commented. 'Anyone could have seen you.'

'Yeah,' Teague agreed. 'If they had, I'd've scrapped the whole idea; tried something else another time. But I knew on Saturday she'd use that cloakroom and the terrace'd be clear.'

'How?'

Teague laughed again. 'Because she'd left her bloody bag of stage make-up in there! I saw it Saturday evening, when that reception was going on in the garden. I went to take the key out of the side-door, so as no one would lock it and bugger everything up for later on. The door to the cloakroom was open and there was a make-up bag on the shelf over the basin. I knew it had to be hers. No one else would bother with tarting themselves up in the middle of the play. So I guessed she wouldn't be hanging about on the terrace. And I was right. I saw her walk off round the side of the house while I was half-way up the lawn. If she hadn't, I'd've done what I'd first thought of, gone round myself by that cloakroom door and risked being seen.'

'And after that the rest was easy,' Finch suggested.

'And quicker,' Teague added. 'I was out of there in a couple of minutes flat. When he saw me come in, he thought the scene by the pool was over.'

It was a brief, laconic statement but Finch could follow its reasoning. As far as Hampden was concerned, Teague's ar-rival through the terrace doors on to the stage was perfectly natural. Seated in the dining-room, out of view as well as earshot of the pool, there was no way that Hampden could have known how far that second act had progressed. When Teague entered, Hampden had assumed it was finished and Teague had returned in readiness to take over the lighting and

184

sound effects for the last act. No wonder he hadn't even risen from his chair, let alone put up a struggle.

As Finch himself had stated, the rest was easy, a simple matter for Teague of taking the curtain cord from its hook and whipping it round Hampden's throat as he sat behind the desk.

In Teague's own words, it had taken a couple of minutes; that was all.

And after that?

At a guess, Teague must have got out of there in a hurry. He couldn't be sure how long he'd have before Annabel Thorpe returned from the cloakroom or Roz Bennet came in from the office to set the stage for the final act. In addition, he'd have to gather up the extension leads, quite a length of cabling if they'd stretched from the pool to the terrace, and disconnect the jackplugs at the end of them from the sockets in the lighting console before hiding them somewhere to be collected later; probably that night, after the team of detectives had left and before a search was made round the pool the following morning.

Once Teague had received permission to dismantle the sound and lighting equipment, he must have thought he was in the clear, and he would have been if McCullum hadn't taken those close-up shots of the console.

As soon as the cables were disconnected and safely hidden, Teague must have hurried back to the dining-room in time to reappear at the terrace doors, giving the impression he'd just that moment arrived from the garden.

It was an ingenious scheme, neatly worked out; not surprising, for that was the way the man's mind worked. Finch had seen enough evidence of that in Teague's workshop. As far as Teague was concerned, the mechanics of the idea would have been easy. He had probably regarded it as something of a challenge, sitting up there alone night after night in that cell-like room, brooding over what he saw as Hampden's betrayal and the uncertainty of his own future should Hampden marry.

Teague had spoken of Clayton's plan to pick Hampden off

with the rifle as he strolled round the garden at Cressetts as nothing more than a game; a mere toying with the idea of murder.

Was that how Teague's own scheme had started? And if it had, at what point had Teague decided it could be played for real?

These were questions which would have to be asked once Teague was disarmed and taken into custody.

As he stood there on the slope of the field, it occurred to Finch that he, Teague, Boyce and the others were engaged in their own game; a waiting game; a game of dare, if you like; the sort that kids play, challenging one other to make the first move, only this time played in deadly earnest.

Teague faced him, still kneeling, the gun held steady and aimed, as Finch estimated with a coolness of judgement which surprised him, at a point about an inch above his right eye. If the man fired, there was a good chance of the bullet going straight through his head and out the other side.

At the same time, he was acutely aware of his surroundings as if all his senses had been scoured clean, allowing him to absorb the smallest details, pin-sharp and newly minted.

Below him lay Cressetts and its garden. He could see the glitter of the water as the sunlight reflected off the pool, the flag-stones of the terrace, almost white against the vivid emerald of the grass and the darker viridian of the bushes and trees. He had never realized quite so consciously how many different shades of green existed. There must be dozens of them.

The sky was almost cloudless, a clear blue faintly marbled with white and somewhere up there in the dazzle a meadow lark was singing, shrill and piercingly sweet.

But it was on Teague he concentrated most of his attention, narrowing it down so that he had the man in sharp focus. The bony head with its dark hair was cocked and held as steady as the gun. One eye was half-shut as it squinted down the sights while the shoulders were stiff with holding that same unchanging pose.

And yet, despite the intensity of his concentration, Finch was not prepared when the man finally moved.

It was over in a matter of seconds.

Teague dropped down on to both knees, at the same time swinging the gun round so that the barrel was underneath his chin. In that brief interval before he pulled the trigger, Finch was certain he saw the corners of the man's lips flicker upwards in a smile which remained there, fixed and rigid, like the stretched grin on the face of a corpse.

The next instant, the gun was fired and the smile disappeared from sight.

He toppled forward on to his face; thank God, Finch thought as he ran towards him, closely followed by the other man who broke from the cover of the wood.

They stood in a silent circle for a few moments contemplating the body before Finch took off his jacket and laid it over Teague's head.

'Sorry,' he said to no one in particular although he seemed to be addressing the dead man. 'It didn't work out.'

Not that he really meant it.

As he turned away, he was thinking that this was probably what Teague himself had wanted – a quick death up there on the hill slope under the open sky.

16

It was Christie who rang Roz first with the news of Teague's confession and subsequent suicide.

'But why him?' she asked. She could hardly take it in. 'What possible reason could he have for murdering Oliver?'

Bewilderment was mixed up with a sense of enormous relief that it wasn't Noel after all, as well as guilt that she had suspected him in the first place.

'It's a long story, Roz,' Christie replied. 'I'll tell you about it some time. At the moment, I'm still down at Cressetts but I'll have to come up to London soon to sort out some business affairs, mine as well as Oliver's. The point is, I wondered if you'd like to meet me for dinner one evening to discuss that plan of mine.'

'What plan?' Roz asked. She had no idea what he was talking about.

'To move the publishing firm down here. You remember? We talked about it in the garden the afternoon before the play. I offered you a job. I wanted to know if you'd be interested in taking it up. Roz? Are you still there?'

'Yes,' she said.

His voice, quick and eager, hurried on. 'It's obviously not going to happen for several months yet. There's still a lot of legal details to settle so there'll be plenty of time for you to give in your notice. And there'll be no problem either about accommodation. There's room over the stables for a flat.'

He's got it all worked out, Roz thought, just as he had that afternoon at Cressetts. And no doubt he's already decided exactly what our relationship will be – me installed on the premises but keeping a low profile whenever his wife turns up for the weekend or his sons for school holidays.

'So what do you say, Roz? Although you don't have to make up your mind right now.'

'I already have,' Roz told him.

It wasn't just the idea of becoming his lover although she knew she wasn't the type for that sort of long-term deception. Nor was it guilt at the thought that she'd betrayed him to Finch.

It was that damned Hampden charm that she mistrusted; that, and the realization that he was more like Oliver than she had imagined.

Christie, too, liked to manipulate others just as his brother had done.

Come into my parlour, said the spider to the fly.

Well, she had no intention of being lured into Christie's web, however soft the blandishments and however tempting the bait.

'Sorry,' she said briskly, not really meaning it. 'I'm going to have to turn you down.'

'You won't change your mind?'

'No.'

'Ring me if you do. The offer's still open.'

She hung up before he did.

Noel phoned about half an hour later with the same news about Teague which he'd heard on the grapevine at work.

He sounded his normal self as if the scene outside his flat when he'd told her to shove off hadn't happened.

But Cliff Teague wasn't the only reason for his call. He was eager to talk to her about something else. Roz could hear it in his voice, that boyish enthusiasm which came bubbling up even through his disappointment that he wasn't the first to tell her the news. He didn't even bother to ask her where she'd heard it.

'Listen,' he was saying. 'You remember we talked about my job and how much I hated it?'

It was evidently going to be an evening of reminiscing, Roz

189

thought, although her recollection of the conversation with Noel wasn't quite how he described it.

No matter. After all he'd been through, Noel needed to protect his self-esteem. She'd do the same if she were in his shoes.

Realizing she was in for a long session, she sat down on the sofa and put her feet up. 'Yes,' she said. 'I remember.'

'Well, I've given it my notice.'

'Noel, you haven't! What are you going to do instead?'

He seemed pleased at her delight and concern. 'Don't worry, I've got that sorted out. I met this girl in a pub; Maggie; absolutely super; very *simpatica*. You must meet her, Roz. You'll like her. She's your sort of person. Anyway, we got talking and it turned out she runs a small theatrical company in Camden; nothing grand; just her and a few part-time actors. They do a lot of pub and fringe theatre and they also tour – small towns, village halls, that sort of thing. She's offered me a job; general dogsbody, really; a bit of producing and stage-managing as well as acting and running the business side. The salary's not very good but there'll be a percentage of the takings.'

'That's splendid, Noel!' Roz said. There was no need for her to fake her pleasure. It was quite genuine.

'You agree I've done the right thing?'

There was an edge of anxiety in his voice. So he really hadn't changed all that much, Roz thought. He was still looking to her for reassurance.

'Of course I do. It's much more up your street than working in an office.'

'You really think so? Seriously though, Roz, I've been wondering for some time now about branching out into something else and when Maggie. . . . '

Swapping the receiver over to her other ear, Roz settled back against the cushions.

Finch also had a call that evening. He had taken home some of